BLOOD OATH

NON-FICTION SECTION BY CHRISTOPHER EDGE

www.pearsonschoolsandfecolleges.co.uk

✓ Free online support
✓ Useful weblinks
✓ 24 hour online ordering

0845 630 33 33

Heinemann

Part of Pearson

Heinemann is an imprint of Pearson Education Limited, Edinburgh Gate, Harlow, Essex, CM20 2JE.

www.pearsonschoolsandfecolleges.co.uk

Heinemann is a registered trademark of Pearson Education Limited

Text © Chris Priestley 2011
Non-fiction text © Christopher Edge 2011
Typeset by Kamae Design
Cover design by Wooden Ark Studios

The rights of Chris Priestley and Christopher Edge to be identified as authors of this work have been asserted by them in accordance with the Copyright, Designs and Patents Act 1988.

First published 2011

14 13 12
10 9 8 7 6 5 4 3 2

British Library Cataloguing in Publication Data
A catalogue record for this book is available from the British Library

ISBN 978 0 435 04605 7

Printed at China (EPC/02)

Acknowledgements
We would like to thank the following schools and students for their invaluable help in the development and trialling of this book:

Croesyceiliog School, Cwmbran
Callum Beckett, Josh Tyler, Ryan Lo, Hannah Evans, Ben Hobby

Huish Episcopi Academy, Somerset
Blake Armstrong, Tom Levett, Ben Lock, Charlie Stamp, Michael Tew, Jack Stephens

For Adam.
Thanks for the help.

CONTENTS

CHAPTER ONE

Raven had heard the story many times but never tired of it. He turned to his mother and smiled, and she in turn smiled back at him, her face glowing in the light from the fire.

Raven's father's voice dropped to the tone he always used when telling the tale. He was sitting on the other side of the fire, which burned in the centre of the round house, and his form shimmered in the haze from the flames.

Sparks danced in the darkness, heading upward with the smoke as it searched for escape. The roof above was as black as night, with sparks for stars. The fire warmed the listeners and lit their eager faces.

'Listen now,' said his father, 'and I'll tell you the tale of how I took the Dragonhead Torc.'

The people of the village clapped and banged their platters at these words. They loved to hear the story as much as Raven did.

As he spoke, Raven's father put his hand to the torc, the great gold neck-band he wore at his throat, which was open at the front and flexible enough to force round your neck. At the ends were two snarling dragon heads.

'I was not your chief in those days,' said Raven's father. 'My father was your lord. He was a great man. Some of you will remember him.'

The older people in the round house murmured and nodded.

'I was a young man then,' said Raven's father. 'Not many winters older than my own boy there.'

Everyone turned to Raven and he blushed.

'It was the time of wars. Our people were attacked by a war party from the high country to the north. Their chief was a great bear of a man. His face and arms were lined with battle scars. He was a good fighter. I'd never seen better – apart from my father.'

Everyone smiled and Raven glowed with pride at the mention of his grandfather.

'My father feared only the gods,' continued Raven's father. 'Some of you greybeards remember him and know I speak the truth.'

The older men and women nodded and mumbled their agreement.

'He walked right up to that warrior and hit him hard across the shield and knocked him to the ground. I thought he'd killed him with one blow and we cheered as we saw the man lying there, his shield in two pieces.

'But in moments the man was back on his feet, a bloody gash across his arms and fury in his face. His red hair looked like fire and his eyes seemed to burn too as he stepped forward and swung his axe at my father's head.

'A slower man than he would have lost the fight there, and his head along with it, but my father was quick, as well as strong, and leapt aside.

'The invader was on to him again. All warriors meet their match one day. This was my father's day. The attacker's axe came again and I heard my father hiss with pain as the blade sliced across his shoulder. The next blow killed him dead.'

A hush fell now as the elders remembered.

'I cried out in pain and anger,' continued Raven's father. 'My rage gave me the strength of ten men, and I ran forward without a weapon, knocking the chief to the floor and sending him sprawling.

'He looked at me as he got to his feet and a smile came to his lips when he saw that I was a boy and had no axe.

'The chief did not want to fight a lad like me and so began to walk away. But I picked up my father's sword and yelled at him. I called him a butcher and a coward and all the foul names I knew. In the end he had no choice but to turn and face me.

'He was head and shoulders higher than me and twice my weight, with arms as thick as my legs. I thought my days were over.

'I knew that I could not match him blow for blow. He was too strong for that. No – I had to use my speed and my wits and hope that they would be enough.

'But he was fast for a big man. I only just managed to save my skull and I wear this scar for not being quick enough. This is where his axe kissed my silly head.'

Raven's father put his fingers to the long pale scar that reached from his hairline to his right eyebrow.

'Almost lost my eye,' he continued. 'And I could hardly see, there was so much blood. The big man moved in for the kill and I knew that this might be my last chance. I said a prayer to the gods.

'I waited for him to come close enough and, as he raised his axe, I lunged forward with all my might and caught him a mighty blow under his jaw.'

The listeners roared as Raven's father mimed the blow.

'I heard the bone break. I felt his teeth judder and crack. Blood spurted from the wound and I remember his face looking down at me, his eyes wide, for he knew it was a death blow. And then I struck again, just above the torc, and his life came to an end like he had ended the life of my father.'

The elders muttered praises to the gods.

'His neck gushed with blood and my hand was red with it as I pulled the torc free and held it high above my head. Our people cheered and waved their axes and spears.'

At this the people in the round house cheered and banged their platters, and Raven cheered along with them. His father's hand moved to the torc and stroked the shining gold.

'I put the torc round my neck, wet with the chief's blood, warm from his battle rage,' he continued over the cries of his listeners. 'I still wear it on feast days like these to show that we were once a great people, brave in battle.'

The cheers rang out again. His father held up his hands and the noise faded to silence.

'My father taught me the ways of a warrior as I have taught my own boy. We have been at peace for many years now, but we must still honour the ways of our forefathers. This is still our land, whatever the Romans may think.'

Angry growls rumbled through the round house. Raven could not imagine a time before the Romans came and built their wall to the south. It seemed so hard – like trying to think of a time before the sun or the rain.

The Romans had always been there. Or that was how it felt to Raven. But there were men in the round house who were boys when the wall was built – wood and earth at first, and then stone. His own father had been a babe when it had appeared, and the milecastles and forts and towns along with it. Nothing would ever be the same again.

Raven was normally excited by the story of the Dragonhead Torc, but it seemed different this time. This time Raven was aware of the sadness that went with it. It was a story about a time long gone.

He got up and walked to the door. He wanted to feel the cold air on his face. It was dark now. He looked up into the sky and at the countless stars scattered across the blackness.

Suddenly, flames began to erupt from the roof of the round house in front of him and, out of the darkness all about him, came the unmistakable shapes of armed men.

CHAPTER TWO

Raven shouted the alarm and men rushed from the round house. As they did, all hell broke loose in the village.

The intruders began yelling at the top of their voices and they seemed to come from all around. They were getting louder too, and quickly closer, as they rushed forward from out of the black and into the glow of the firelight as yet another hut went up in flames.

Spears flew from the darkness, clattering off walls and thudding into thatch and flesh. Raven felt the breeze of a spear blade as it sailed past his ear.

Raven's father yelled orders and the village men searched for their weapons. Raven's father strode forward: axe in one hand, sword in the other. One of the attackers rushed at him, but he struck him in the ribs so hard he almost split the man in two.

All around there were cries of anger, cries of pain. Swords and axes clanged together, sparks flying in the darkness.

And then Raven saw him. He could see by the way the man walked and moved that he was the leader of the attackers. Even the smoke seemed to part as he came forward; Raven seemed to see nothing else.

His hair was long and even in that poor light it glowed red. He was pale-skinned and strongly built, his arms painted with coils of deep blue. He was like something from the legends – the ghost of the warrior Raven's father had killed.

But he was no ghost. Raven's father saw him too and made straight for him, yelling and swinging his axe. The attacking chieftain dodged the blow, though only just.

Someone grabbed Raven's arm and tried to pull him away. It was his uncle.

'No!' said Raven. 'I have to stay. My father –'

'Your father himself told me to take you to safety and I will do it even if I have to carry you.'

'But the fight!' cried Raven.

'The fight is for men,' said his uncle angrily, 'and you are a boy. Your time will come. Do you not think I'd rather be fighting than being your wet nurse? I'm too old, and you're too young. Now come on!'

Raven looked back as he was pulled away. The invader and his father were fighting blow for blow, but he could see that it was his father who was moving forward and the attacker who now seemed always to be on the back foot.

But then he noticed another of the attackers moving behind his father. He carried a spear and watched the fight like a wolf, waiting for his chance to spring.

With Raven watching in horror, the man crept up behind his father and rammed the spear into his back. 'No!' shouted Raven.

Raven's father cried out in pain and turned to face this new attacker. And as he did so, the chief saw his chance. With one mighty swing of his axe, he struck Raven's father in the back with his axe.

'No!' screamed Raven again as his father fell lifeless to the ground.

Raven pulled free of his uncle's grasp and rushed forward. He would avenge his father just as his father did all those years before.

But no sooner had he begun to stride towards the leader of the attackers than his uncle grabbed him and pulled him back.

Raven struggled and swore, striking out at his uncle, but his uncle was stronger, putting his hand over Raven's mouth to muffle his shouts and dragging him away into the darkness.

Raven became aware of others in the darkness and recognised his mother's face. Her tear-filled eyes met his and he stopped his struggles, hugging her and joining her sobbing.

Raven's uncle whispered directions and the group moved away from the village. Raven burned with shame as he realised that the group was made up of elders, women and children. Once again he tried to go back to the village and the fight.

This time it was his mother who held him back. She shook her head and her eyes pleaded with him to stay. Raven closed his eyes but all he could see was his father falling to the earth and his killer's grin of triumph.

'Do not leave me alone in the world,' said his mother, leaning towards him.

Raven opened his eyes and saw his mother's face inches from his. He bowed his head and after a moment nodded in agreement. All strength seemed to have gone from his legs. He felt dizzy.

They escaped in the darkness, edging along the west river – the glow from their burning village casting shadows of trees on the opposite bank, the fires flickering along the water.

The war whoops of the invaders gradually died away as the villagers made their way further and further from their home, never resting until they stood, shivering and sobbing, on the shores of a wide black lake.

CHAPTER THREE

Few of the villagers slept. They huddled together for warmth and comfort until dawn broke and the lake slowly turned silver under the light of the new day.

Raven watched, still numb from the night before, as two of the elders went to check the village. After a while they returned to say that the attackers had gone and that it was safe to return.

The survivors walked slowly, no one eager to see what they knew they would find when they came back to their houses.

All their worst fears were confirmed. The small round houses were blackened, like burnt bread. The bodies of their fighting men lay all about, and each body soon attracted a mourner – a wife, a mother, a daughter.

Raven's mother had seen her husband fall, just as Raven had done, and made straight for his body. Raven thought it best to let her go first, but as she approached she fainted and fell to the ground.

Raven rushed to help her and saw for himself the grim and pitiful sight of his father's body lying on the ground.

Again he was sick with anger and shame at not having avenged his death or died in the effort.

But there was worse to come. As he approached, it became clear that the invading chieftain had not only killed his father – he had taken his father's head as a trophy. Raven felt like he was falling into a deep pit and had to steady himself.

They would have to say farewell to him that way. But how could a man go on to the afterlife without his head? He would roam the dreams of the living, moaning for justice. He would never rest.

The funeral pyre was made and Raven joined his uncle and the elders in choosing the wood and piling it in the meadow.

Then they carried Raven's father, wrapped in a blanket woven by his mother, to the place of burning and put his body on top of the wood stack. Raven himself lit the flame.

How hungry the fire seemed. It roared up through the woodpile, crackling and hissing. Within moments the whole pyre was alight and so hot that Raven's tears were dry before they had barely left his eyes.

They stood and watched the flames swallow the warrior's body and his mother and the other women wailed a keening song. When at last the whole thing collapsed, the men joined the women and they all chanted the song of the dead and asked the gods to take his soul to the place of feasts and good hunting.

Slowly the mourners moved off. Even Raven's mother eventually allowed herself to be led away. But Raven would not budge. He stood alone, staring at the red embers.

'I swear on these ashes,' said Raven, 'that I will avenge your death or die in the attempt.'

Raven took a knife and let its blade bite into his arm and drip on to the ashes.

'I swear by my blood,' he said. 'I promise you. I make this blood oath to you, Father, and I hope you forgive me for my cowardice.'

At that moment a breeze suddenly blew and swirled the ashes into a tiny whirlwind, spinning them round and round and up into the air. The embers glowed an even hotter red.

'Father,' said Raven, wide-eyed, 'is it you? Are you angry with me?'

'Look after your mother,' said a voice he recognised in an instant.

'*Father?*'

'Raven?' asked a voice behind him. He turned to see his uncle. 'Are you all right?'

'Yes,' said Raven. 'I was … I heard …' Raven stared at him, confused, and then gazed back into the fire.

'Come on, lad,' said his uncle. 'The living need you.'

'Do they?' said Raven doubtfully.

'It is a time for us all to be together. Your father would expect you to do what is best.'

They gathered enough material to re-roof one of the houses and all the survivors huddled together, happy to have the closeness and comfort it brought. When night came, the men took turns guarding the village, and Raven insisted that he should take his turn alongside them.

Dawn broke on his watch and the sky turned pale green above the dark horizon. A new day was a hopeful thing. But not this new day.

Later that morning each of the surviving members of the village took a handful of the ashes from the funeral pyre and put it in a pot.

The pot was handed to Raven, who carried it to the barrow, the resting place of all the village chiefs and the place where Raven's grandfather's ashes were laid to rest.

Raven put the ashes in the pit, placed his father's axe alongside it and filled it in. Then the entranceway was sealed once more with piles of rocks and clumps of turf and the ancient stone carved with coils and circles.

As soon as his father was buried, Raven called the people together amid the ruins of the village and his uncle called for them to listen. They looked frightened and confused and Raven suddenly felt nervous himself. He tried to remember how his father would have spoken at such a time.

'A great wrong has been done to our village and to our chief!' he said when he stepped forward.

He tried to sound bold as his father would have done, but his voice came across as weak and thin and seemed to drift away like smoke in the cold air.

There were nods and some muttered agreement, but it was not the enthusiastic response he had hoped for. Raven felt small all of a sudden.

'My father gave his life for you,' said Raven. 'What will you give in return?'

The villagers looked at each other. A baby began to cry. Jackdaws croaked as they flew past and gathered in the trees at the stream's edge.

'We cannot just let these murderers come into our village and kill our people!' said Raven.

'What do you expect us to do?' asked an old man. 'We are not of a fighting age. Our fighters are dead and buried. We are farmers now. All we have is a ditch to stop the animals from wandering. What if they come back?'

'My father went to the aid of other villagers in the past,' said Raven. 'We fought for the village at the three hills. Remember? We can join forces with them and –'

An old woman nodded her head.

'The boy is right. We should ask them to take us in,' she said. 'They still have a hill fort.'

'Aye,' said another. 'The three hills village is a nice place. The people there are friendly and the river is full of fish.'

'No!' shouted Raven. 'We cannot just leave *our* village. This is the place of our people. This is our land. We need to avenge our dead!'

'Where were you when the fighting raged?' shouted an old man.

Several people tried to hush the old man but he waved them away.

'It is easy for this boy to stand here and say we should fight for our land,' he said. 'He is a boy. We are farmers now, not warriors. Those days are gone.'

Raven blushed with shame and looked at his uncle. There was no fight in his face either. His uncle reached out to him but Raven shrugged him away and walked towards the stream.

He gazed out on to the moor where he had learned to ride. He was a good rider – better even than his father had been. But the invaders had taken all the horses and Raven's stallion, Storm, along with them. His whole world seemed to have been robbed.

Hunger brought him back to his people. The smell of cooking drifted towards him on the cool evening air. The men had put a roof back on the round house and a fire was burning as Raven entered.

His mother looked up at him with tears in her eyes and he could not look at her. He felt ashamed of himself and ashamed of his people. He wished with all his might that he had joined the young men in the fight and died alongside them. There was pride in a death like that. To live on like this was only a half-life.

CHAPTER FOUR

When Raven rose the following day, he noticed that some of the elders were already standing in a huddle with his uncle. His uncle was nodding, but sadly.

Raven walked towards the men, who grew silent at his approach and slowly began to walk away. His uncle looked across the hillsides towards the Roman wall. When he turned back to Raven, the boy could see the tears in his uncle's eyes.

'The elders have spoken,' he said.

'Uncle?'

'We can't stay here, Raven. We must –'

'The elders should have spoken to me,' said Raven. 'My father was chief here and I am his son.'

'Your father won the right to be heard,' said his uncle. 'He won that right through bloody combat.'

Raven's uncle put a hand to his face and ran it over his eyes. When he turned back, he looked tired and older somehow. His voice was quieter.

'The men who attacked us come from the north,' he said. 'We have heard they are attacking the Romans.'

'The Romans?' said Raven. 'If their fight is with the Romans then why do they attack us?'

'They are wild, Raven. They see us as weak because we farm and trade with the Romans.'

'Maybe they're right!' said Raven.

'You're a boy, Raven, and we are old men, women and children. We have no choice. What can we do?'

His uncle's words about combat had stung Raven, but he did his best not to show it.

'I don't know, but I won't go,' said Raven. 'This is our land. This is my land.'

His uncle nodded.

'That is your choice, lad,' he said. 'You are thirteen winters now and you must go your own way.'

Raven's mother was standing at his side. Raven's uncle bowed to her.

'I will not go either,' she said.

'But –' began Raven's uncle sternly.

'Do you think you can bully me into going?' said Raven's mother. 'You've known me too long.'

Raven's uncle nodded and smiled and reached out to touch her shoulder.

'Then may the gods be with you,' he said.

Raven's uncle walked away, leaving Raven and his mother standing alone. Raven could not meet her gaze. He felt angry and sad and confused.

'You should go,' said Raven without looking at her. 'Father would have wanted –'

'Don't tell me what your father would have wanted,' said his mother sharply. 'I think I know that as well as anyone.'

Raven hung his head. Tears welled in his eyes and he felt like his heart would choke his breath. His mother put her hand under his chin and lifted his face.

'Do you think I would leave you?' she said. 'I have lost my husband. Do you think I could leave my baby here alone?

Raven smiled. 'I'm not your baby any more, Mother.'

'You will always be my baby,' she said. 'As long as I am alive.'

Tears fell from Raven's eyes and he began to sob. He was filled with shame that he should cry in front of his mother at his age, but she pulled him towards her and they hugged until the sobs fell away.

'I'm too soft-hearted,' said Raven. 'Too soft to be a warrior. I wish I was more like my father.'

'Ha!' said his mother. 'That's *where* you get your softness from. Your father was as a gentle man as he was a warrior. *I* was the tough one.'

And Raven knew at once that this was true. He remembered many occasions all at once when it had been his father who had dried his tears and asked his mother not to be so hard on him.

'Your father had the courage to be gentle when gentleness was needed,' she said. 'A warrior without a heart is a butcher and nothing more.'

Raven nodded, but he was no warrior, soft-hearted or not. What use was he? How would they cope alone in the village? Raven's mother seemed to read his thoughts.

'But we cannot stay here,' she said.

Raven frowned.

'We cannot leave Father's grave,' said Raven bitterly.

His mother grabbed his arm.

'Your father was a fighter,' she said. 'But he would not want you to waste your life. You could have done that last night. He wanted you to live.'

Raven looked up at the sky. The brightness of it hurt his eyes.

'It wasn't for him to say. I should have fought to save him,' he said. 'I should have tried to kill his murderer.'

'And if you had,' she said, 'you would have died for sure. What good would that do anyone? What good would it have done me?'

Raven looked at his mother. 'Then what are we to do? Where are we to go?'

His mother looked away to the south and then back to Raven.

'We will go to the strangers.'

'What?' said Raven. 'The Romans? No! I won't go there!'

Raven could not believe his ears. Was his mother really suggesting that they go to live with the invaders?

'Yes you will,' said his mother. 'We will be safe there. *You* will be safe there.'

'But, Mother –'

'You will obey me as you would have obeyed your father,' she said. 'This is my wish. I have sold my cloth to the strangers before. Now I will live among them and do the same.'

Raven opened his mouth to speak but could think of nothing more to say.

He felt exhausted. What right did he have to argue? He could offer no alternative. His mother was right. They could not stay there alone and he was not going to follow his uncle and the elders. His pride would not allow it.

He would start a new life among the Roman strangers. Maybe that was the punishment the gods had given him for allowing himself to be dragged away like a coward instead of dying a noble death.

CHAPTER FIVE

Raven and his mother made their way along the track that led up to a ridge which looked out across a wide plain.

The sky was dark above them and a chilly wind blew in their faces. Running along a craggy ridge, like a snake on the horizon, was the wall.

It was not the first time Raven had seen it. They had taken things to sell to the soldiers of the fort and the town that lay beyond it. But each time he saw it, it sent a shiver through his bones. Each time he marvelled at how mere humans could have made something so huge and so vast, stretching away from dawn in the east to dusk in the west. It seemed like the work of gods.

It took them a day of walking to reach the gates and they only just got there in time before the gates were shut for the night. The Roman guards were rough and rude and spoke to Raven's mother as though she was a slave, but his mother had warned him to say nothing and he obeyed.

The contrast between the wide empty land they had left and the noise and bustle of the fort was amazing.

No sooner were they through than the gates closed behind them. Soldiers barred the gates with a great piece of timber and Raven could see the sentries above the wall, torchlight shining on their helmets, javelins and body armour.

They walked through the fort, its soldiers' barracks and stables all laid out with alien regularity. Raven was used to curves and coils. Everything here was straight and squared off. It made Raven uneasy. It did not seem right.

They passed through the fort to the town that had grown next to it. The locals who lived here had long ago decided that they might as well accept that the Romans were here to stay. Besides, the soldiers were bored and looking for ways to spend their wages. The townsfolk were only too happy to help.

Raven's mother sold a gold bracelet to pay for food. Raven held one of the coins they received in his hand. It had a face on it – a Roman face.

'That's their chief,' said the man who bought the jewellery. 'Or it's their old chief. Marcus Aurelius has just died, so they say. There's a new emperor now. He's called Commodus.'

'Commodus?' asked Raven, looking at the coin. Raven looked around the fort. 'He must be a rich man. Where does he live?'

The man laughed. 'He doesn't live here, you young fool. He lives in Rome. It's a city far away to the south.'

'A city?' repeated Raven, puzzled.

The man chuckled again.

'Goodness me, but you've a lot to learn,' he said. 'These Romans come from a place many, many days away. Beyond the sea. Beyond the land beyond the sea.'

Raven knew there was a sea to the east and to the west. His father had bought a shell from a traveller and given it to him when he was younger. But he did not know that there was a sea to the south.

'They say that their lands stretch in all directions as far as any man can travel,' said the man.

The man seemed lost in these thoughts for a while and Raven could not imagine what that meant, for he had never travelled more than a day in any direction from his home. What lay beyond had never been his concern.

'One day they will own everything,' said the man coldly.

Two Romans walked past as he said this, and the man immediately stepped away from Raven and busied himself about his shop as if he had said nothing at all.

Raven turned to his mother and she smiled weakly and said that they ought to find somewhere to stay. Raven was hungry and he could see that his mother was very tired.

They found a lodging house that also served food and, as they sat at a bench near the fire, the warmth of the fire made him sleepy.

They had already paid for a room in which to spend the night and the owner came over and asked what they would like to eat. He had a kind voice and Raven liked the way he spoke to his mother. He treated her with respect.

They ate well. It was not the food he was used to, but Raven liked it well enough. But the number of people in the town made him nervous. He did not like crowds. Every few seconds he would hear the voices of people walking by and would look up nervously from his food. His mother touched his hand gently.

'It's all right, Raven,' she said. 'We're are safe here.'

Raven was not so sure. There were so many men here and in the fort. Men meant drinking, and drinking meant fighting. He was in no mood to relax.

Things were not improved when four Roman soldiers came in. They took their helmets off and put them noisily on the tables beside them.

They spoke loudly in their strange language and Raven wondered what they were talking about. One of them turned to look at Raven and then back to his friends. They all started laughing and Raven felt the blood rise to his face. Were they making fun of him?

'Raven,' whispered his mother, 'pay no heed to them.'

Raven muttered something and scowled.

'We are in their land now, son,' she said quietly.

Raven knew that was true, but he did not have to like it. He stared back at the Romans, silently hating their loudness and their laughter.

This is still my land, he said to himself. *You can put a fort here and you can build your wall, but it will always be my land and you will always be the enemy.*

Their room was clean and quiet, and soon Raven could not keep himself awake any longer. When he opened his eyes, daylight was seeping between the wooden shutters and his mother was standing, smiling down at him.

'Come on,' she said. 'No time to lie around all day.'

They went to see a man to whom Raven's mother had sold cloth before. She hoped that he might be able to help, but it was clear within minutes that he was not interested in them.

He was a red-faced and rude man. Raven recalled him from an earlier visit and remembered why he had not liked him. His opinion had not changed.

They returned to their lodging with heavy hearts, unsure of what they might do next. The few coins they had from selling their wares would not last long. They had to find some way of earning more. They sat silently at a table and the owner came across to ask why they had such long faces.

'You're a weaver?' he asked, when Raven's mother explained.

'Yes,' she replied.

'Any good?'

Raven's mother scowled, got up and began to walk away.

'Steady there,' said the man with a chuckle. 'Don't be like that. Sit down. Please.'

Raven's mother sat back on the bench.

'Do you have anything to show me?' asked the landlord.

Raven's mother unrolled a long cloak with green and brown stripes overlapping to form a check. The man whistled appreciatively.

'That's fine work,' he said.

'You know about cloth then,' said Raven's mother.

'I know enough to tell good stuff when I see it.'

'You won't see better than this.'

Raven's mother smiled and winked at Raven. He had never seen his mother like this.

'What would you say if I offered you a place to work?' asked the man.

'I'd say, what's in it for you?' asked Raven's mother.

The man laughed. 'Well,' he said. 'I'd charge you a rent – a reasonable one, mind – and you'd have a place to live with your boy here. But mainly I want to attract a better class of customer to this end of town.

'The soldiers have money and nothing much to spend it on but gambling, women and drink. But there's any number of places they can do that. I'd like to offer them something else. Something with a bit more class. Maybe a nice shawl to send back to their mothers. What do you say?'

Raven's mother looked at her son and he looked at the man and back to his mother. Raven nodded and his mother agreed.

'A mother who looks to her son before making a decision,' he said. 'Why's that then?'

'This boy is a chief,' said Raven's mother. 'He is a warrior's son.'

The man nodded. 'A warrior's son, eh?' he said, looking at the coiled tattoos that snaked up Raven's arms. 'But are you ready to work?'

'I'm not lazy,' said Raven.

'Good,' said the man. 'Then I'll see what I can do. I don't need a warrior, but I can always use a hard worker.'

Raven nodded and the man walked away. His mother reached out and grabbed his hand tightly, smiling.

'You see?' she said. 'The gods have not abandoned us.'

Raven smiled, but he wondered to himself whether their gods even knew they were here, whether their gods ever crossed that wall.

CHAPTER SIX

The landlord was as good as his word. The workshop he rented to Raven's mother was perfect and in no time at all Raven's mother was well known throughout the town.

Soldiers came from the fort and bought her cloth and told their friends, who came as well. The workshop was always busy. Months passed.

The landlord would say again and again that the day he met Raven's mother was the best day of his life. Not only was her weaving business thriving, but his tavern had never been busier.

He treated Raven as though he was a nephew or a grandson. Raven had sullenly resisted this as much as he was able, but the man's good honest nature was often too much for him.

Raven quickly got the hang of running the tavern, and even though he was just a young lad, he soon got to know all the customers and knew the ones to smile at and the ones to avoid when they got drunk.

The owner trusted him completely and Raven was grateful for that trust. It helped to ease the pain he sometimes felt that he, a chieftain's son, was carrying jugs of ale instead of a battleaxe.

Two winters passed: one hard and long. The old man got ill and Raven had to run the tavern single-handedly while his mother weaved by day and looked after the owner in the evenings.

When he recovered, the old man was convinced that they had saved his life and his business. Raven thought they probably had.

Raven and his mother became settled in the town. His mother was so successful that she could employ two young women to weave the work she did not have time for.

Raven worked hard too and was given more and more responsibility by the old man. Carrying jugs of ale and wine every night had put some muscles on his arms and Raven had become a powerful young man – not as powerful as the Roman soldiers who came in, yet still he could see that they did not look down on him quite so much now.

Raven watched the easy way that his mother had with these young men. It surprised him. He had always thought of her as shy. But these soldiers were not so much older than he was and they no doubt missed their mothers.

Raven was fascinated by these soldiers: by their accents, their weapons, their armour. Some of them became friendly with him, joking with him when they saw him, and sometimes they stayed and talked about the lives they had left to come here. It was not just the ordinary soldiers, but the Spanish cavalry whom Raven loved to watch train their horses and the dark-eyed archers from Syria.

There was one soldier in particular who seemed to take a shine both to Raven and his mother. Raven recognised that he had the same warrior bearing his father had had.

He was a big man but he had a quiet voice and a gentle manner. He would stop by most days and chat. Raven could see that he was dressed differently from most of the soldiers in the camp and asked him why.

'I'm a centurion,' he replied.

'What's that?' asked Raven, frowning at the unfamiliar word.

'It means I'm in charge of a troop of men – about eighty of them. They are good men, most of them. Young and homesick – but then aren't we all?'

The centurion asked Raven's mother to make a shawl for him and she agreed.

'Is it for your wife, sir?'

'No,' said the centurion. 'I have no wife.'

'Oh,' said his mother with a smile that made Raven frown.

'I had a wife once,' said the centurion after a pause. 'And a son. He was about your boy's age the last time I saw him.'

'Had?' said Raven's mother.

'She died,' he said, taking a deep breath. 'And my boy along with her. There was a plague in my homeland and … well, it was a long time ago.'

'I'm sorry,' said Raven's mother. 'Would you marry again?'

The centurion shook his head. Raven frowned at his mother again, wondering why she was so interested in this Roman.

'This is no life for a married man,' said the centurion. 'I would not want to leave my wife for years on end and what wife would want to live in this …' The centurion paused, realising that he was about to insult their homeland.

Raven's mother laughed. 'Is it so much nicer where you come from? Is it so much nicer in Rome?'

'I'm not from Rome,' he said. 'Few of the men are. I come from a country called Dalmatia.'

'Is Dalmatia so much nicer?'

The centurion smiled. 'I think so,' he replied, 'but it has been so long. Maybe the place I dream about does not exist any more. Or maybe it never did.'

When the centurion left, Raven glared at his mother so long that she stopped what she was doing and turned to him to ask what was wrong.

'Why were you flirting with that Roman?' he asked.

'I was not flirting with him,' she said. 'I was talking to him, that's all. I like him. He's sad, I think, and a little –'

'He's a Roman!' said Raven angrily.

'Lower your voice,' hissed his mother. 'We need these Romans now, whether you like it or not.'

'That doesn't mean we have to like them,' he said. 'Look what they've done to our land.'

'It wasn't Romans who killed your father and burned our village!' said his mother.

Raven stared at her for a few moments and then turned and stormed off to the edge of the town and beyond – into the meadow near the blacksmiths and pottery kilns.

He sat under a tree looking back towards the town and the fort and the wall that stretching out to either side.

Raven knew his mother was right but he suddenly felt trapped and tamed. It was as though he had been a wild horse and now he was a donkey – a well-fed donkey, but a donkey all the same.

When he got back to his mother's workshop, she was with a customer. Raven waited until the man left and put his hand on his mother's shoulder.

'I'm sorry,' he said. 'I should not have spoken to you in that way.'

When she turned, he could see that she had been crying. Her eyes were red.

'No,' she said coldly. 'You should not have.'

CHAPTER
SEVEN

Things changed after that day. Bit by bit, little by little, Raven came to accept his fate. He did sometimes yearn for the life he felt had been taken from him, but those times became fewer and fewer.

He had sad days too – days when the memory of his father and of his friends and neighbours and their old life in the village would come back to him in a sudden unexpected burst – but they seldom made him cry now.

Raven would not have described himself as happy, but he was not unhappy. He surprised himself by realising that he was fairly content with his life.

But then one day this newfound contentment came to a sudden and horrible end.

Raven's mother had to take a couple of blankets to the fort and, since it was getting late, he said that he would go with her. He did not like her walking alone at night and it was not too busy at the tavern. The old man was happy to be left alone.

Raven's mother delivered the work and they started home. Raven no longer felt the fort to be alien, but he was still happy to leave its gates and return to the town.

'I know that it is not the life you thought we would have,' said his mother. 'But we are happy enough, aren't we?'

Raven smiled. 'Yes, Mother,' he said.

It was true. Things could have been much, much worse. But still Raven could not help thinking that this was not what he had been brought to the world to do. His mother seemed to sense his thoughts.

'This is not warrior's work,' she said.

'Protecting my mother from harm?,' said Raven with a grin. 'There is nothing I'd rather be doing.'

'Truly?' said his mother.

'Truly,' said Raven.

They walked on. Shops were closing and locking their doors. Lamps were being lit and fires were fed with logs. There was a chilly breeze in the air and the smoke from the roof holes swirled as it rose. The summer was coming to an end.

His mother stumbled and Raven just caught her before she fell.

'I'm getting old,' she said with a laugh.

'You work too hard, Mother,' he said.

Suddenly, Raven was barged into and knocked off his feet, and he ended up lying against a stable door. When he turned round, he saw three men surrounding his mother. Raven saw the flash of a knife and leapt to his feet. One of the men had already grabbed his mother and was demanding her purse.

Raven picked up a broom that was propped up against the stable and snapped the shaft under his foot, leaving a sword-length piece of wood.

The nearest robber laughed as he saw Raven approaching but didn't see the blow that knocked him out.

The second robber was quicker, though, and managed to block the blow that came for him with his staff, hitting back at Raven with a winding strike to the boy's ribs, making him drop his weapon. Raven staggered back, and the man lurched forward, aiming the end of his staff at Raven's face, but the boy managed to grab the staff and shove it aside. He stepped forward and landed a punch to the robber's kidneys, making him groan with pain. Raven kicked his feet away, sending him crashing to the ground. Raven kicked him in the side of the head as he was getting up, and the man lay still.

The third robber was still struggling with Raven's mother.

Raven heard her scream and she turned to Raven and stared wide-eyed, reaching out a hand to him. Then she dropped to the floor.

The robber stood over her: a purse in one hand, a bloody dagger in the other.

'Mother!' yelled Raven.

The robber turned to face Raven as the boy ran towards him, but Raven was too fast. His fury had given him strength and he crashed into the robber, sending him tumbling; the two of them rolled around in the dirt.

Suddenly, there were soldiers all around them. One of them grabbed Raven and hauled him to his feet. They tried to get the robber to stand too, but he would not move. The dagger he had used on Raven's mother was now sticking out of his ribs.

Raven tried to go to his mother, but a different soldier struck him in the stomach with the hilt of his sword, making him crumple and sink to his knees, gasping for breath.

'Easy, soldier,' said a voice he recognised through the pain. It was the centurion.

'He's killed a man, sir,' said another soldier. 'We need to take him to the prison.'

The centurion looked at the body and then at Raven.

'My mother, sir,' whimpered Raven.

'I'll look after her, lad,' said the centurion.

The two unconscious robbers were doused with water and kicked awake. They were dragged away.

The centurion knelt down beside Raven's mother and lifted her head. As he brushed aside her hair, her eyes opened.

'Don't move,' he said. 'I'll fetch a doctor. We have a Greek here and he is like a magician. He'll –'

'Too … late,' said Raven's mother. 'Dying.'

Raven struggled to come forward but was held fast by a soldier. The centurion took a deep breath. He knew it was true and the last words a person hears in this life should not be a lie.

'I am so sorry,' he said.

'Look … after … Raven,' she whispered.

'Your son?' said the centurion looking at Raven. 'I don't know that –'

She grabbed his arm. 'Please!' she said, her face ugly with pain.

'All right,' he said. 'I'll see what I can do.'

At that, her face relaxed and her hand fell away from his arm. He laid her head gently on the ground.

'No!' shouted Raven, struggling again to break free of the soldier.

The centurion nodded and the soldier let Raven go. He dropped to his knees and pressed his face against his mother's hair, sobbing like a child.

The centurion gave Raven a few moments and then put his hand on the boy's shoulder. Raven turned to face him, his face wet with tears.

'I'll take care of her,' said the centurion.

Raven nodded. A soldier reached down to grab his arm but Raven shrugged him off and got to his feet, going with him without a fight.

'You!' called the centurion to a nearby soldier as a crowd began to gather round them. 'Fetch two men and have this woman carried to my house. Make arrangements for a funeral. She was a chieftain's wife. Treat her with respect or I will have you flogged.'

'Sir!' the soldier barked and marched away.

CHAPTER EIGHT

Raven sat in the gloom of his cell trying to ignore the taunts of the robbers who were locked up in the cell next to him. For hours they had been threatening to kill him in ever more painful ways.

But Raven didn't care. He was barely listening to them. His father was dead and now his mother was too. He had nothing left in the world and wanted only to die himself. He did not care how.

'Shut up!' said a loud voice. Raven looked up slowly.

The centurion was standing outside the robbers' cell. The light from a burning torch flickered across his armour.

'One more word from either of you and I'll have your tongues cut out. Do you understand?'

The robbers grew silent. The centurion wandered slowly towards Raven's cell and stood looking through the bars. Raven ignored him.

'I am sorry about your mother,' he said. 'She was a good woman.'

Raven said nothing.

'I have arranged for her funeral myself,' he said. 'She will be treated well, I promise you. Prayers will be said to the gods for her.'

'Not her gods,' said Raven.

The centurion sighed and looked away. Raven stood and began to walk back into the shadows of his cell.

'I will try to put in a word for you with the commander,' said the centurion.

'What about us?' asked one of the thieves.

'I've warned you already, scum,' the centurion barked. 'Don't make me say it again!'

He moved closer to Raven's cell. 'I think I may be able to help you. You were acting only to protect your mother.'

'Don't bother,' said Raven. 'I don't want your help.'

'Even so,' said the centurion. 'I am going to give it – if only for your mother's sake.'

Raven started to argue, but the sound of marching feet quieted him as the commander arrived at the cells with his guard.

'Commander!' said the centurion, standing to attention and saluting.

'Calm yourself, Marcus,' said the commander. 'Just out for a stroll and thought I'd pop in. Who do we have here?'

The commander peered first at the two thieves and then at Raven.

'As you know, sir,' said the centurion, 'we arrested three men today in connection with a theft and the murder of a woman from the town.'

'There was another murder, was there not?' asked the commander.

'The man who was killed was himself the murderer of the woman. He was a robber, sir.'

'You are sure?'

'There were several witnesses, sir,' said the centurion. 'The boy who killed the man was the woman's son. And he –'

'This boy?' asked the commander, looking at Raven.

'Yes, sir,' said the centurion. 'I know him. He's a good lad. He was only trying to protect his mother – as any boy would. The woman was a respectable weaver. You have employed her yourself, I think. She worked –'

'Are you saying that this boy was right to take the law into his own hands?'

'No, sir,' said the centurion. 'I am merely saying that he had just cause to –'

'Because we have Roman law here, Marcus,' continued the commander. 'It is fair and just and we can't have any little barbarian boy thinking he can –'

'But, sir …'

'My goodness, centurion,' said the commander. 'I almost thought you interrupted me. But I know that you would never do that, would you?'

'No, sir,' said the centurion.

Raven could hear a trace of bitterness in the centurion's voice, but if the commander noticed it he did not show it.

'Crucify them,' said the commander with a sigh.

'Sir?' said the centurion.

'You heard me, man,' said the commander, looking at Raven and raising an eyebrow. 'You served in Judea, just as I did. You know what a marvellous effect that has on the local people. Crucify them.'

Raven had no idea what 'crucify' meant, but he could tell it was nothing good.

'But, sir,' said the centurion, 'we do not do that here.'

'Really? Well, it seems like a perfect time to start.'

'Is it, sir? There have been several attacks on the wall already. Do we want to make more enemies?'

'That is exactly why we need to be strong, Marcus,' said the commander looking down his long nose at Raven. 'Look at him. He'd stab you in the back as soon as look at you. Force is all these people respect. And it would not do any harm to remind the troops how the enemies of Rome are treated.'

The centurion frowned.

'Come, Marcus,' said the commander, lowering his voice. 'Don't look at me like that. You know as well as I do that there have been rumblings of discontent among the legions. I won't tolerate it here.'

'Of course not, sir. The men are loyal to Rome. I promise you.'

'But are they loyal to me, Marcus?' whispered the commander.

The centurion bowed his head. Raven could see that he was having difficulty finding a reply. 'I have no reason to doubt it, sir,' he said.

'Have the arrangements made, Marcus,' the commander said and turned to leave. But as he was walking away, the centurion called for him to wait.

'Yes, what is it?' asked the commander crossly.

'Well, sir. I agree that crucifixion is a very good way of showing the natives who's in charge, but I just wonder if we might do something a little more entertaining.'

'Entertaining?' said the commander. 'In what way?'

The centurion moved a little closer and dropped his voice. 'We are a long way from Rome here, sir.'

'We are a long way from anywhere here,' said the commander wearily.

'But that does not mean we cannot show that we are still Romans,' continued the centurion.

The commander frowned. 'Go on,' he said.

'We could crucify these peasants,' said the centurion, pointing at the cells.

Raven scowled.

'They will make a lot of noise for a while and then they will simply feed the crows. I think we could have a little more fun with them.'

'I'm listening,' said the commander.

'Why don't we have them fight for their freedom? Have them fight to the death? The one left standing at the end is the winner and can go free.'

Raven looked at the thieves, who looked back, grinning.

'Free?' said the commander. 'I don't like the sound of that.'

'Oh yes, sir,' said the centurion. 'It will show how powerful you are and how fair. Nothing shows that more than giving the gift of life.'

The commander nodded. 'Yes – like the gods themselves,' he said.

The centurion raised an eyebrow but though Raven saw it, the commander did not. He was lost in his thoughts of greatness.

'And I do like the idea of a spectacle,' he said. 'Everyone loves gladiators, don't they? A fight to the death. Excellent!'

The centurion saluted and the commander left with his guard. The centurion turned to Raven, staring at him for a moment before following the commander out.

'Do hear that, boy?' said one of the thieves to Raven. 'We are going to cut you to pieces.'

Maybe, thought Raven. *Or maybe not.*

CHAPTER
NINE

The day of the contest approached and the centurion had persuaded the commander that the combatants needed to have some instruction in fighting as gladiators or it would end too quickly.

The two robbers and Raven were stripped to the waist and taken to an open area near the wall.

'The commander has been soft-hearted enough to let you filthy scum fight for your freedom,' lied the centurion. 'If it was down to me, I'd have you all killed here and now and save the empire the expense of training and arming you for this fight.' The centurion turned and slyly winked at Raven. 'But the commander has instructed me that you should be trained so that you provide fitting entertainment for us.'

'Why should we fight for you, Roman?' asked one of the thieves.

'Give him a sword,' the centurion said to one of his men without looking at the robber.

The soldier handed his sword to the robber, who gripped the hilt and stared at the centurion who now walked towards him, unarmed.

'You hate Romans?' said the centurion. 'Well, come on then. Now's your chance.' He opened his arms.

The robber did not move.

'Come on, coward,' said the centurion. 'Or is it only women and boys you fight?'

'If I cut you, they will kill me,' said the robber, nodding towards the soldiers.

'So you value your life then?' asked the centurion.

'Of course.'

'Then that is why you will fight. The gods have seen fit to grant you scum a chance to live, when by rights you should all be nailed to a cross, feeding the crows. If you fight, you may live. If you don't, you will surely die.'

The centurion walked closer towards him and opened his arms wide again. 'Or you can die here and take a Roman with you,' he said. 'If you think you can.'

The robber seemed to weigh up this idea for a few moments before throwing the sword to the ground.

The centurion grabbed him by the throat. 'From now on you will do as I say without question,' he said, 'or you will enter the arena with only one hand!'

He let go of the robber, who sank to his knees, gasping for air.

'Train these men,' the centurion said over his shoulder as he walked away. 'Wooden swords, mind. We wouldn't want them cutting themselves.'

The training began. Each prisoner was paired with a soldier. Each was given a wooden sword.

At a command, the soldiers lunged at the prisoners, who defended themselves as best they could.

The soldiers paired with the robbers found it simple to break down their defences. Neither man had ever used a sword. Swords were expensive and they needed skill. Knives and clubs were more their style.

So the soldier paired with Raven took one look at the youth in front of him and grinned. Raven clenched his teeth. The swords were wooden, but they would still hurt.

The soldier rushed forward, shoving his sword towards Raven's guts. As he ran at him, Raven jumped sideways to avoid the thrust. The soldier had put all his power into the movement and almost fell flat on his face.

The soldier turned and saw Raven standing firm: legs apart, head down, ready for a fight. The soldier muttered something about luck. The centurion walked back just at that moment.

Raven grinned. He saw the centurion and thought he would show him what a warrior's son could do.

As the soldier moved towards him a second time, Raven ran forward to meet him, sword above his head, aiming to bring it down on the soldier's head.

But he had only run three steps when the soldier dropped to one knee and thrust his wooden sword into Raven's stomach.

Raven gasped in pain and fell to the ground, grasping his stomach in agony. The soldier walked forward and kicked him in the legs. 'You think you're a match for me, do you, peasant?'

He was about to kick him again, when the centurion came over. The soldier saw him coming and stood to attention.

'That'll do,' said the centurion. 'I think the prisoner has learned his lesson.

'Sir!' said the soldier.

Raven could see that everyone had stopped and the robbers were looking over with broad grins on their faces.

Raven got to his feet, rubbing his stomach to ease the pain.

'Carry on,' said the centurion. He stayed and watched for a while.

Raven continued with the training, but the result was always the same. He was sure that he should be able to be better than these soldiers – his father had taught him how to use a sword and his father was a great warrior. He grew more and more frustrated and, by the time they returned to their cells, his confidence was gone and he was nursing several black bruises.

Two soldiers marched into the prison an hour or so after they came back and said that the centurion had ordered that Raven be brought to him.

'Perhaps he's going to kill you himself and save us the bother,' said one of the robbers.

Raven went with the soldiers to a courtyard outside the barracks. The centurion was waiting for him. He told the soldiers to leave and tossed Raven a wooden sword.

'Try to hit me,' he said.

'No,' said Raven. 'I'm tired.'

'Better tired than dead,' said the centurion. 'Come on. My hands are empty.'

The centurion held up his hands to show this was true. The frustrations of the day finally boiled over in Raven and he rushed at the centurion, aiming a blow at the side of his head.

In a move so quick Raven did not even see it, the centurion blocked Raven's sword arm, grabbing his wrist, while his other hand took his sword from its scabbard and held it to Raven's throat. He could see his own startled eyes in the shining metal blade.

'If you fight like that in the arena, you will die,' he said.

Raven said nothing.

The centurion moved closer and dropped his voice to almost a whisper. 'Your father trained you well. You have the skill to stay alive, but you must not fight with anger. Anger will blur your sight and slow your hand. I've seen it too many times. Fight with your head, not your heart.'

Raven looked into the centurion's eyes with all the defiance he could muster but he could not hold the centurion's gaze. He looked down at the ground.

The centurion called for the soldiers. 'Take him away. Lock him up again.'

A soldier grabbed Raven's arm and began to lead him away.

'Wait,' called the centurion. He walked over and stood in Raven's path. 'Those robbers have stolen your mother from you,' he said. 'Don't let them steal your life as well.'

The centurion nodded to the guard who led Raven back to his cell. The robbers grinned as Raven was shoved back inside.

'You're going to die tomorrow, country boy,' said one.

'So are you,' said the other robber.

'We'll see about that,' said the first.

'Shut up, all of you,' said the guard, banging on the bars with a stick.

Raven sat in the corner of his cell and closed his eyes. The centurion was right and he knew it.

CHAPTER TEN

The announcement of the fight had caused much interest in both the fort and the town. The soldiers had not seen gladiators for a long time, while most of the townsfolk had never even heard of them.

An arena had been cleared just outside the town. Soldiers forced the crowd into a large circle to act as the boundary. Children squirmed through them to get a view, but older and wiser heads kept their distance, aiming to keep clear of the fighters and their swords.

It was a bright summer's day. Raven squinted up into the sky and wondered if this would be his last day. If it was, he thought, then he must be brave and die with honour.

The sunlight glinted on the helmets and spears of the soldiers on the wall's ramparts as Raven was led into the arena, the crowd parting to let him and the robbers in.

It was then that Raven noticed the wooden tower that had been erected at one side to allow the commander to have the best view.

The centurion was waiting for the commander's signal and when it came he stepped into the arena. 'By the generosity and charity of our commander, you have been given the chance to win your freedom or die a warrior's death in the effort,' he shouted.

The crowd cheered. Raven's mouth felt very dry all of a sudden. He had been warned to stay still until ordered to move, but he looked around without moving his head. There was a pile of weapons in the centre of the arena. They would be led to the centre of the arena and armed, he thought. But he was wrong.

'At my signal, you will come forward and take your weapons. Anyone who moves before my signal will be shot.' The centurion pointed towards three Syrian archers.

'As you see, you will have to choose your weapons,' he continued. 'There are two swords and one spear. There are two shields and one helmet.'

Sword and shield, sword and shield, Raven said to himself.

'When I drop my sword,' said the centurion, raising it in the air, 'the fight begins and you must gain your weapons by any means you can.'

The crowd cheered again.

'Remember this is a fight to the death,' he said. 'Only one of you can leave this arena.'

The centurion raised his arm a little higher. Sunlight seemed to run along its length like molten silver. He looked towards the commander who nodded and the centurion dropped his sword.

Raven launched himself forward but, as he did so, the robber to his left punched him hard in the ribs, knocking the wind out of his lungs and sending him tumbling in the dirt.

By the time he got to his feet the robbers had already picked up the swords and shields and had turned to face him. If they fought as a pair, Raven had no chance.

But as the first man stepped towards Raven, the other robber hit his one-time comrade across the shoulder with his sword, making him yell in pain and turn to his attacker.

Raven saw his chance and dived at the spear and helmet before the nearest robber could stop him. Raven thought about putting the helmet on but decided that it would be more use as a makeshift shield. As he wrapped the chinstrap round his hand, he saw the centurion nod with approval.

Blood was pouring from the wounded robber's back and he winced and cried out every time he moved. He was in pain but his anger carried him forward, hacking at the other robber.

However, his blows were wild. Raven tried to distract the other robber. But even as he tried to do that, the injured robber turned and lunged at him, almost catching him with his sword.

Raven cursed himself for being such a fool, but before the words were even out of his mouth, the other robber struck his former comrade a savage blow between the shoulder blades.

The robber cried out, his eyes staring at Raven in shock and horror. Then he fell face down in the dirt.

As the remaining robber turned to the crowd celebrating his win, Raven picked up the dead man's sword and spun to face his opponent.

The crowd became still. They knew that they were about to witness the end game.

'Give up now, boy,' said the robber. 'I'll kill you quickly. You have my word. Give it up and I'll take you down with one blow. You won't know it's happened.'

'Your word?' said Raven angrily. 'You think I'd take your word? No more words. Come and kill me if you can.'

The robber needed no further invitation. His sword point whistled as it carved the air, missing Raven's nose by inches.

Again the sword sliced the space between them and again it came close to slicing Raven's face along with it. Raven made no attempt to block its path.

'Is that the best you can do?' taunted Raven.

The robber scowled and lurched forward. Raven sidestepped and struck him on his sword arm, just above the elbow.

The robber hissed in pain and anger and lunged again. He was quicker than Raven thought and almost caught Raven in the stomach. Raven just managed to swat the blow away with the helmet.

He remembered what the centurion had said. He must keep calm. He must think clearly. One mistake and his blood would be seeping into the dirt.

The robber came again. This time Raven struck him and the robber knocked the blow away with his shield. But before he could use his sword, Raven struck him a fierce blow across the side of the face with the helmet.

The robber did well to stay on his feet. He shook his head and blinked, spitting out a tooth and a spout of bloody spit. His eyes widened in fury.

This is it, thought Raven. *This is it.*

The robber roared and rushed forward, his sword arm raised above his head and his shield ahead of him. Time seemed to slow down. Raven felt calm. He felt the spirit of his father by his side.

As the robber was about to bear down on him, Raven dropped to the ground and threw out his legs, sweeping the robber's feet from under him and sending him tumbling through the air. The robber landed on his back, and before he could get up, Raven threw himself forward, sword in both hands and rammed the blade through the man's chest, pinning him to the earth. The robber twitched once and died.

Raven rolled away, exhausted. His skin was covered in the blood of the two men. He slowly got to his feet and looked at the centurion, who walked towards him and nodded to the commander. Raven understood what he meant and turned to the commander, raising his bloody sword in salute.

The commander stood and raised his arm in return. 'You have fought bravely,' said the commander. 'By the glory of Rome, I grant you a pardon for your crime.'

Raven bowed his head, threw down the sword and pushed his way through the crowd, who patted him on the back and cheered. He felt sick. He just wanted to get away.

Suddenly the centurion was by his side. 'Come on,' he said. 'This way.'

CHAPTER
ELEVEN

Raven stood in the centurion's house and looked around. It was smaller and emptier than he thought it would be. The walls were bare except for a small alcove where there was a shrine.

'Is that your god?' asked Raven.

The centurion looked at the alcove with its small stone figure. 'One of them,' he said.

'Thank you,' said Raven quietly. Then after a long pause. 'For helping me.'

'That really hurts you, doesn't it?' said the centurion with a smile.

Raven frowned deeply. 'I'm grateful for what you have done for my mother,' he said. 'And for the help you gave me.'

The centurion nodded. 'Crucifixion is the worst death there is,' he said. 'It can take days to die, the crows feeding on you while you are still alive. I felt that you deserved a fighter's death at least.'

Raven nodded.

'What will you do?' asked the centurion.

'I don't know,' said Raven. He was feeling restless. What did this Roman want with him?

'How will you live?'

'What do you care? Why are you taking this interest in me?'

'I liked your mother,' said the centurion. 'I like you. You remind me of my son. And you remind me a little of myself at your age. I didn't always wear this uniform you know.'

Raven stared at him. What did this Roman know about him? Nothing. What right had he to say he was like him?

The man continued; 'I am a Roman now, but once I came from a small village, a village not so very different from yours, I would wager.'

'Where?'

'A long, long way from here,' said the centurion sadly. 'Another world.'

Raven looked away, annoyed at how upset he suddenly felt. 'At least you have a home to go back to. I have nothing.'

The centurion walked forward and put his arm on Raven's shoulder.

'Why not enlist?' asked the centurion.

'What?' said Raven, pulling away.

'Join the army,' said the centurion. 'What else are you going to do?'

'I don't know.' Raven turned to walk away.

'I ask you again – what else are you going to do?'

'Go back to the tavern and carry on working there.'

The centurion nodded and raised an eyebrow. There was something about his expression that Raven found annoying.

'And you like that work?' asked the centurion.

'Yes,' said Raven, hearing the lie in his own voice. 'I'll be all right. I'm not becoming a Roman, I know that!'

The centurion cursed under his breath and grabbed Raven by the arm. 'You are a brave lad,' he said. 'But you have no control. Without family or friends you will get into trouble. I've seen it before. I can't save you twice.'

Raven shrugged him away. 'I don't need someone telling me what to do,' he said. 'You're not my father!'

The centurion nodded. 'You're right,' he said. 'I'm not.'

Raven started to walk away.

'But,' called the centurion, 'if I were your father – if you were my own son – I would tell you the same thing.'

Raven headed back to the town and arrived at the tavern to find the doors locked and bolted. He banged on the wood and called out to the owner, who eventually appeared from an upstairs window.

'Who's there?' he called.

'Me,' said Raven. 'Let me in.'

The old man came down and unlocked the door. He seemed tense and nervous, almost as if they were strangers again.

Raven walked over to the dying fire and warmed himself in front of the embers. He began to tell him about the fight but the old man said he did not want to hear about it.

'What's the matter?' asked Raven.

'You have to leave,' he said.

'What?'

'I'm sorry,' said the old man. 'But I can't have trouble here.'

Raven frowned.

'A man came from the commander and said that if I carried on employing you then he would take my licence. I'm sorry.'

Raven kicked a chair over, sending it clattering across the tiled floor. 'My mother made you rich, you old coward,' he said.

'I know,' said the owner. 'But I'm old and the old have to be cowards. I'll pay you well. It's the least I can do.'

'Keep your money,' said Raven. 'To think we saved your life. We should have let you rot.'

The old man hung his head in shame and when he lifted it again Raven was gone and the door swung open like a gaping mouth.

Raven wandered out into the meadow next to the town. It was night now, but it was clear and there was enough of a moon to see by. He could even make out the sentries on the wall by the dull glow of their moonlit armour.

He closed his eyes tightly, his head spinning. He cursed his fate, cursed the old man and cursed the whole world

that had led him to this sorry place. Then he got up and
walked towards the fort.

The centurion turned to see Raven standing in the doorway.

'How do I do it?' asked Raven. 'How do I become a
soldier? How do I start?'

'You just did,' said the centurion.

CHAPTER
TWELVE

The centurion was not joking. He called a guard as soon as they had finished speaking and Raven was taken to the barracks and shown a bed.

The guard barely spoke to him and the men in the barracks watched silently as he walked past. Then they turned back and ignored him completely.

Raven lay on his bunk and closed his eyes. The fight seemed like a lifetime ago, but suddenly he felt exhausted. Within seconds he was asleep.

And it felt as though only seconds later a soldier was smacking him on the leg with a stick to wake him up.

Raven shot upright, ready for a fight. The soldier grabbed his sword hilt and smiled. It was the same soldier who trained him for the arena.

'Any time, peasant,' he said. 'Any time.'

Raven took a deep breath and backed down.

The soldier laughed. 'Get dressed. Food's downstairs if you're quick.'

Raven got dressed. He had been given his kit the night before and he slowly put the unfamiliar clothing on and went down to the canteen to eat.

Most of the soldiers in the fort seemed to be in there. Raven thought the place might go silent as he walked in, but no one even seemed to notice him.

He walked to the serving counter and a very fat cook ladled some porridge into a bowl and handed it to him with a slab of bread.

Raven took it to a table with a space and sat down. The soldier nearest to him turned and realised he was looking at a new face. 'New boy?' he said.

'Yeah,' said Raven.

'Do as you're told and you'll be all right,' said the soldier.

Raven nodded. He had not asked Raven's name and Raven did not offer it or ask his. 'Is that what you did when you were new?' asked Raven. 'Did as you were told?'

The soldier shook his head and leant forward to show him a scar on his forehead. 'That's how I got this,' he said.

The soldier nodded towards the centurion – Raven's centurion – who was sitting with the other centurions at a long table near the window.

'He did it,' said the soldier.

Raven frowned.

'He's a mean one,' said the soldier, getting up with his empty bowl. 'But the best damn soldier you'll ever meet.'

The training began. Raven was taken out into the area where he had fought the thieves.

The low sun was bright and it hurt his eyes. There were three other recruits standing with him. They were all older than he was, but not by much. They all looked scared. Raven realised he probably did not look any different. None of them knew what to expect. An officer strode forward and showed them the back of his hand where there was a tattoo of an eagle.

'This is the legion's mark,' he said. 'If and when we decide you are good enough to be a member of the legion, you too with have this mark. But only if you deserve it. Get ready to start your life in the army!'

Raven was no stranger to weapon training. He was a chieftain's son, and even though the glory days of his people were behind them, Raven's father still wanted his son to know something of the old ways.

Raven's father had taught him how to use an axe and a sword, a shield and a bow, how to move and dodge. They trained with lengths of wood for swords and axes and his father would even let Raven hit him from time to time, though Raven knew that he was only letting him. His father was far too good to ever be caught by a boy like him.

These memories came flooding back as Raven stood waiting for his training as a Roman soldier to begin.

He and his father had trained on the meadow beside the curved river, and though his father had worked him hard, there was always laughter and kind words.

Raven could tell that there would be no kind words here. The Romans seemed a joyless lot once they put their armour on. He had seen them laugh and sing at the tavern, but here they seemed altogether different.

Raven and the other recruits were told that serving in the Roman army was a great honour and that it was only open to those who worked hard, trained hard and learned well and quickly. They were going to be put through their paces to find out what they already knew – if anything.

It started well enough. Raven surprised his trainer with his ability with a javelin, but Raven had been throwing a spear since he could walk. He had killed his first deer when he was eight years old and the elders had marvelled at how far he had been from the animal when he hit it.

Raven enjoyed the praise he got and happily ignored the scowls of the other recruits who had clearly never thrown a javelin in their lives.

The trainer called some soldiers over to watch as Raven threw again and they clapped at his skill. The soldier from the canteen was there and he nodded at Raven and grinned. Whatever he had been expecting, this was better. Raven forgot himself for a while and smiled.

But it was not to last. The soldiers moved on to sword training and again Raven impressed his trainer. He had learned from his brief time as a gladiator and put his training to good use.

But he was not as good as he thought he was. His trainer caught Raven with a heavy blow to the ribs and

Raven lost his temper completely, flying at the man and raining blows at his head.

Other soldiers had to step in and restrain him and he struck one of them in the face. The officer in charge hit him hard in the stomach, making him sink to his knees, all the wind knocked out of him.

'Pick up that stone,' said the officer.

Raven looked at where the soldier was pointing and saw a stone about the size of a loaf of bread. He frowned.

'Pick it up! Now!'

Two soldiers moved forward, hands on sword hilts and Raven put his hands up and moved towards the stone. He leant down and picked it up.

'Hold it in both hands above your head,' said the soldier.

Raven did as he was ordered.

'You will hold that stone above your head until we tell you to drop it,' said the soldier. 'If you drop it before you are ordered to, you will be beaten and made to carry it again. If you drop it twice, you will be beaten and thrown out of the fort. If you try to return, you will be killed on sight. Do you understand?'

'Sir!' said Raven.

CHAPTER
THIRTEEN

The centurion walked to where Raven was standing holding the stone. It was dark now. Raven did not know how long he had been standing there. The centurion told the guards to leave. Raven fought to stay awake.

'Look at you,' said the centurion. 'Do you think anyone cares that you are here?'

'No, sir,' said Raven, tasting the salty sweat that dribbled into his mouth as he spoke.

The centurion sighed and turned away and Raven could tell that he was trying to keep his temper. His father used to do the same thing. The centurion turned back to face him.

'In the end you will either be a Roman soldier or you will be dead,' he said. 'Is that it? Should I have let them crucify you?'

Raven did not respond.

'Listen to me,' whispered the centurion. 'They will not waste punishment after punishment on you. I can't help you if you will not help yourself.'

'I never asked you to, sir,' said Raven.

'I've seen men die through punishment beatings,' said the centurion. 'This is just a warning.'

'Sir!'

The centurion cursed and clenched his fists. 'Why fight for your life in the arena only to die like that?'

'Perhaps it's better this way,' said Raven, fighting back tears. 'Maybe it's better that I die. I don't want to live like this …'

The centurion moved closer, his face more gentle now. Raven could feel the Roman's breath on his face.

'None of us have the life we want,' said the centurion quietly. 'I have not seen my family for six years. Do you think I want to be here in this windswept hole?'

Raven did not answer but stared straight ahead.

'Do you not think I would rather be sitting with my family and friends, listening to the old stories in my own language?'

A tear trickled down Raven's face and he winced with the effort of holding the stone, closing his eyes tightly. When he opened them again, the centurion had stepped back.

'You will either be a soldier or die in the effort,' said the centurion calmly. 'And if you are not a good soldier then you will die in the first combat you face.

'Let them train you, boy. We do not know what the future may bring. But this is the best that the gods have given you for the present. It could be a lot worse.'

Raven blinked away the sweat of concentration. It was hard to focus. He was so tired. His arms hurt so much.

'There is no point fighting,' said the centurion. 'If you are going to fight a fight you cannot win, then let it be a glorious fight on which your ancestors will look down with pride. Do not waste your life like this.'

After a moment Raven nodded. The centurion took the stone from him and Raven was amazed to see how small it was.

He hissed with pain as he put his arms down.

The centurion smiled and clapped his hands on his shoulder. 'The next time you disobey an order I will kill you myself,' he said.

'Yes, sir,' said Raven.

Chapter
FOURTEEN

'You are leaving a great hole in the defence,' shouted
the officer.

Raven wanted to shout, 'Then they should come with
me and fight like men!' But he had promised himself that he
would not argue, so he nodded and tried again. The results
were always the same, though.

Ever since the day of his punishment of holding the
stone over his head, Raven had been a very different recruit.
Everything he was asked to do he did with an energy that
surprised everyone around him.

He was fearless in every combat exercise. He was always
first to the fight and every blow he took was a lesson learned.
But though no one could have faulted his energy, Raven still
fought his battles as though he was a lone warrior.

Of all the aspects of becoming a Roman soldier, the
idea that you fought as part of a disciplined group of men
was the most difficult for Raven. He was an army of one. It
did not feel natural to be part of a team.

They were practising a defensive move called the
tortoise – the soldiers would line up behind shields, some
holding them over their comrades' heads for protection.

Raven did not even know what a tortoise was, and even if he had he would not have seen it as something to copy.

What kind of warrior hid behind a massive shield and jabbed at the enemy from his hiding place? When all the men were in place, the shields covered everything. It was a coward's way of fighting and he felt ashamed to be part of it.

'No, no, no!' yelled the officer.

Raven stopped in his tracks and tried to hide his frustration. 'Move with the group! Move with the group!' he repeated to himself.

But again and again, when the order came to move into position and defend themselves against another group posing as attackers, Raven left the group and began to fight back on his own.

It was no better when they were training to form the wedge – a pointed formation led by one man that was used to jab through an enemy attack. Again Raven would break loose as they attacked.

'Normally we have a problem with men running away,' said the officer, shaking his head. 'You're the other way round. But we'll just have to go through all again until you get it through that thick head of yours, won't we?'

Raven became more and more frustrated and he could also sense that the other soldiers were getting annoyed with him. They knew that he did not feel he needed them and felt their big shields to be cowardly.

He was sitting on his own during one of their breaks when the centurion came up and set next to him.

'I hear that you are not getting along with the tortoise,' he said.

'I have tried, sir,' replied Raven sulkily.

The centurion smiled.

'I didn't get on with it either when I first joined the army. It feels … cowardly.'

'Yes!' said Raven. 'It does!'

'But it's not,' said the centurion. 'It takes more guts to stay in that formation than it does to rush out, sword flashing.'

Raven frowned. 'How's that, sir?' he asked.

'Because it takes guts to risk your own life for the men around you. More guts than it takes to risk your own. When you get that, you'll get the tortoise. And you'll be a better soldier.'

He got up and began to walk away. After a few steps he turned back. 'Maybe you'll even be a better man.'

CHAPTER
FIFTEEN

Raven entered the barrack block. The men suddenly went quiet at his approach. He frowned, suspicious that they had been talking about him.

'Don't mind him,' said one of the men. 'He hates everyone.' The men laughed. 'Come here, Raven.'

Raven walked over and sat down. He was wary. For all the posing, he knew when men were scared and he could smell fear here.

'My brother is stationed not twenty miles from here,' said one of the men. 'It's the same. There aren't enough men there either.'

'There have already been attacks,' said a soldier sitting next to Raven. 'They're trying to keep it quiet, but it was pretty bad, they say. They're led by a red-haired chief called Redwing –'

'Red-haired?' asked Raven.

'You know him?' said one of the soldiers. 'You come from that lot, don't you?'

Raven shook his head. 'He's not my people.'

'My father sent me a letter from Rome,' said another.

'You should hear what he says is going on there. We are risking our necks up here while Commodus and his creatures feast and lay about all day.'

'Why should we show loyalty to a man like that?' asked the first soldier.

'My father talks about Marcus Aurelius,' said the second soldier. 'Now he was an emperor any man would be proud to serve. I remember when –'

Raven got up, the legs of the bench scraping on the floor.

'What's the matter with you?' said one of the soldiers, grabbing his arm. Raven stared at him until he let go.

'Can we trust you?' asked another soldier.

Raven did not reply.

'I asked you a question, coward!' shouted the soldier.

Raven turned to him slowly. 'I have no interest in this talk. It has nothing to do with me.'

'What makes you so special?' asked a soldier.

Raven shrugged and walked away.

'Let him go,' said one of the soldiers. 'I've seen plenty like him in my time. He thinks he's a warrior. He'll die in his first battle, mark my words.'

Raven sat down on his bunk and then lay down, closing his eyes and ignoring the soldiers as they carried on their conversation. Eventually he fell asleep.

The next morning, Raven walked down to the canteen and could see that he was being ignored. He had never been one for talking to anyone over breakfast, but even so, he could tell that there was bad feeling about the night before in the barracks.

When he tried to sit down, soldiers deliberately filled any available space. Raven smiled wearily and walked over to the table where the archers sat and settled himself there.

Soldiers and archers never mixed. The archers had different gods and looked very different from the ordinary Roman soldiers. They looked up at Raven as he sat down but did not speak to him. The other soldiers nudged and pointed.

Afterwards Raven went outside and was startled by what he saw nearby. One of the archers who had left ahead of him had been knocked down by a huge black horse in the field by the barrack.

The horse snorted and shook its head, rearing up and flicking out its hooves at anyone who came close. The archer was trying to get up.

Raven shouted to him as he strode across towards him. 'Don't move! Stay still!'

The horse turned at the sound of Raven's voice and ran at him. Raven only just managed to jump out of the way as it ran past.

Raven ran to the archer and helped him up. There was blood dripping down his face and he had a nasty-looking bump on his head, but Raven was sure he would be fine.

'That horse is a devil,' said a soldier nearby.

Raven handed the archer to a comrade and to everyone's surprise walked off in the direction of the horse, which was still bucking and rearing and shaking its mane.

The horse's flanks were shiny with sweat and it suddenly put its head down and galloped in a wide circle, the sound of its hooves like a roar of thunder.

Raven walked into the field and stood as still as a statue. The horse turned its head and glared. Then it began to run straight at him.

The horse's hooves hammered the earth and Raven felt the breeze as it passed only inches from his face, its swishing tail slapping his arm as it went by.

Raven did not move. The horse turned and ran at him again. It passed even closer this time, its muscled flanks brushing against Raven and almost knocking him over.

Soldiers began to gather now to see what would happen next. Someone shouted for Raven to come back before he got trampled but Raven did not move.

He began to talk quietly, as though to himself. The soldiers could not hear it, but the horse could and its ears twitched at the sound.

The horse galloped towards him again but, this time, as it approached it slowed down and came to a stop in front of Raven. It snickered and snorted and shook its head and mane. All the time, Raven was gently talking.

Raven slowly raised his arms and the horse – nervously and slowly – walked forward, letting Raven stroke its neck and head until it nuzzled into his side.

The soldiers stared in amazement and none more so than the centurion, who had come over to see what all the fuss was about.

Their amazement only increased when Raven grabbed hold of the horse's neck and in one swift movement hauled himself on to the stallion's back and set off around the field.

Raven rode the horse over to the soldiers. The centurion stepped out and patted the horse on the flanks. It seemed at peace now.

'So you ride?' asked the centurion.

'Since I was a boy,' said Raven.

'You didn't feel the need to say?' said the centurion with a smile.

'You didn't ask, sir,' he replied.

'You are full of surprises,' said the centurion. 'They tell me you saved the archer's life. I thought you only looked after yourself.'

Raven smiled and clicked the horse on, riding it back to the stables as though he rode it every day.

CHAPTER
SIXTEEN

Raven seemed to have only one same dream. He wondered if he had others, but the only one he remembered when he woke was a dream about the night his village was attacked.

In his dream he saw the attackers once again enter the village. He saw the houses burn. He heard the screams of the children and the cries of the women.

He saw the men of his village rush out once more to fight the invaders. He was pulled away by the old men and he fought and fought to stay.

He saw his father meet the invading chief in combat. Each time he saw the fight he was sure that his father would win. This time! This time he would win.

But every time it was the same. The axe would flash through the air and Raven would hear the sickening sound that seemed to have burned itself in his ears – the sound of the axe hacking into his father's neck.

In every dream he tried to close his eyes before he saw the head cut loose and loop through the air, but he never did.

Raven was dreaming this again one night in October when the dream took a different turn. Just as the invaders attacked his village, he seemed to be awake in the fort, hearing the cries of his comrades.

It took Raven a few moments to realise that he really was awake. He saw firelight shining in through the window and it lit up the men in the barracks as they rushed this way and that, getting dressed and strapping on their sandals.

'We're under attack!' shouted a voice outside the door.

Raven got dressed and ran to the armoury with everyone else. A flaming arrow flew past his ear and he felt the heat from the flame. It landed in a building and he ran to pull it out and stamp out the flame before carrying on to the armoury where he strapped on a sword and grabbed two javelins.

Invaders were scaling the walls and climbing over the ramparts. Suddenly, the gates crashed open and a horde of attackers stormed in, followed by chariots with archers on the back.

Raven leapt forward and stood in the path of a chariot as it thundered towards him on wooden wheels. Just before the horses reached him, he hurled a javelin between the horses' heads and hit the driver in the chest, knocking him backwards. The chariot lurched sideways out of control and fell over, throwing the archer against the wall of the barrack block. Before he could stand, Raven was on to him, jabbing his sword between his ribs.

'Where's your armour?' shouted a voice nearby. It was the centurion.

'No time, sir!' shouted Raven.

'You're a Roman soldier, not a –'

But before the centurion could speak, Raven launched a javelin and it whistled straight past the centurion's ear. A cry behind him made the centurion turn round to see one of the invaders at his feet, Raven's javelin sticking out of his gut.

The centurion looked back to Raven and nodded his thanks before grabbing hold of the javelin. The attacker squirmed in pain on the ground. The centurion gave the javelin a sharp twist and the man gasped and lay still.

The centurion pulled the javelin free and went over to Raven.

'Come on,' he said. 'Get a shield. You need to learn, boy. Don't rely on courage or good luck.'

A burning arrow thudded into the wall behind them. The centurion pulled it out as an attacker ran towards him wielding an axe. Before Raven even moved, the centurion had driven the still burning arrow into the man's chest.

The centurion grabbed Raven and shoved him towards the armoury as another chariot rumbled past. This time Raven grabbed a shield.

'Soldiers!' shouted the centurion. 'To me!'

The soldiers in hearing distance all came to the centurion's cry, and he barked a volley of orders, which they all obeyed in an instant.

The centurion organised the men into a shield wall and they stood blocking the path of a chariot. The archer in the chariot fired two arrows as they advanced but both hit shields rather than men.

At the last second, as the horses were almost on them, the centurion barked an order and the wall parted, allowing the chariot through. But as it did so, the soldiers hacked at the horses and men on the chariot. The horses screamed as they galloped and fell sideways, dragging the chariot with them. The soldiers ran forward and finished off the driver and archer.

Another chariot headed towards them. Again the centurion barked his orders and three men walked forward holding javelins. They leaned back and hurled them through the air.

One of the horses fell, a javelin sticking out of its neck, and the other horse kicked its legs in panic, throwing the chariot and the men inside to the ground and running off into the night.

Raven was ordered forward with three other men and they were at the invaders before they had even recovered from the fall.

Raven's mind was reeling. The centurion called them back and they marched to where a group of attackers were setting fire to their storeroom.

Raven could feel his heart pounding and his hands sweating, but he was surprised that he also felt calm and clear-headed.

They hit the attackers before they even realised they were there. It was short and savage, and within moments they were stepping over the dead and looking for their next fight. More of the soldiers were armed now and beginning to form into small groups like theirs. The attack was starting to break down.

It was then that Raven saw him. He would have recognised him anywhere. There on the back of a chariot, rolling past the distant stables, was his father's killer – the golden Dragonhead Torc glinting in the firelight. Without thinking, Raven broke rank and moved towards the chariot.

'Soldier!' yelled the centurion when he saw him. Raven ignored him.

The centurion grabbed him by the arm and turned him round. Raven took hold of his sword hilt and glared at the centurion.

'Pull that sword and I'll gut you here and now,' said the centurion.

Raven relaxed his grip on the hilt and stared back at the chariot.

'What is it?' asked the centurion. 'What's the matter with you?'

'That man,' said Raven. 'He is their leader.'

The centurion stared at the chariot and its red-haired driver. 'They call him Redwing. But I decide where we –'

'He killed my father!' cried Raven.

The centurion sighed. Raven began to walk on, but the centurion grabbed him again.

'He is on a chariot, surrounded by his bodyguards,' said the centurion. 'If you attack on your own, you will die.'

'I don't care!' said Raven. 'As long as I take him with me!'

But as they spoke the chieftain flicked his reins and called his men to retreat.

'No!' shouted Raven as the attackers began to disappear into the night.

Raven grabbed a javelin and started to run. The chariot picked up speed, disappearing behind a building.

Raven ran to try to catch up with it. It came out from behind but was lost again before Raven could throw the javelin, going out of sight behind the barrack block.

The next time Raven saw it, the chariot was heading out of the fort with two others, the surviving raiders running behind. They were swallowed up by the night and Raven slammed the javelin into the ground in frustration.

Suddenly, one of the barbarian stragglers was running straight at him, axe above his head and murder in his eyes. He was so close there was nothing Raven could do but curse.

But the axe blow never came. Just as the attacker was about to bring the weapon down, an arrow struck him in the heart and he dropped to the floor, dead before his body hit the ground.

Raven turned to see the archer he had saved from the horse. The archer nodded to him and Raven nodded back. And then both men went their separate ways to deal with any invaders who were left in the fort.

CHAPTER
SEVENTEEN

Daybreak lit up a scene of destruction. Smoke still coiled up from damaged buildings, their roofs caved in and their walls fire-blackened. Everyone in the fort looked exhausted.

All the able-bodied men from the fort and the town were set to repairing the buildings and salvaging what food and equipment they could from the damaged buildings.

Raven helped to clear burnt timbers from where part of the barrack roof had collapsed. The wood was still hot. Carpenters were already at work on the repairs.

In the afternoon they were all gathered together to wait for the commander, who strode out to take their salute and climbed a wooden platform to deliver his speech. Raven noticed for the first time what a short man he actually was.

'The barbarians who attacked us must be caught and punished,' said the commander. 'No one must be allowed to attack Rome and go unpunished. When one Roman is killed, the whole of Rome mourns their death.'

The townspeople behind the soldiers cheered.

'These savages must be hunted down and dealt with. I myself would lead the raiding party, but my officers have told me that they will not allow it. I am needed here at the fort. But, by Jupiter, I wish I could go with you.'

Silence greeted this statement and the commander frowned at the response until the centurion started cheering, joined a fraction later by the rest of the soldiers. The commander smiled and waved.

'You heard the commander,' said the centurion. 'We will leave the fort and head into enemy territory.'

None of the men spoke, but there was a shifting of feet and a nervous movement of arms against armour. They looked anxiously around. Where were the other centurions? The other men?

'The commander cannot spare many soldiers,' said the centurion. 'We must not leave the fort unguarded. Therefore it will be a small force – on foot – and I shall lead it.'

A soldier near Raven muttered to his colleague. 'No archers, no cavalry. This is a suicide mission. No one who goes will come back.'

'I would prefer volunteers,' continued the centurion.

There was a very clear silence after this statement. They all knew what was being asked and they all knew that if no one made a move, the centurion would simply pick his men anyway.

Raven stepped forward. The centurion shook his head.

'Not you,' he said, pointing back to the line.

'But I wish to go, sir,' said Raven.

'You are a new recruit,' said the centurion. 'You will get your chance to fight when the time comes.'

'I choose this fight, sir,' said Raven.

'You don't get to choose,' said the centurion. 'Rome will choose.'

'Sir,' said Raven. 'I'm a good fighter. I know that land. I was born there. If you go without a guide, you and all these men will never come back alive.'

The commander stepped forward. 'The boy speaks sense, centurion,' he said. 'And I for one feel humbled that a new recruit like him would feel such loyalty to the Empire. I order you to accept him!'

The centurion took a deep breath. 'Very well, sir,' he said with a salute.

The commander left and the centurion turned back to his men. 'Anyone else?'

After a moment's pause the whole century of men stepped forward. The centurion smiled and shook his head.

'Very well,' he said. 'The commander has called for reinforcements and has promised to send some after us when they arrive. But I wouldn't count on it.'

As they were leaving, the centurion walked up to Raven. 'Listen to me, soldier,' he said. 'If you think that you are going to use the Roman army to get revenge on the man who killed your father, then think again! This mission is for Rome, not for you. Do you understand?'

'Sir,' said Raven.

The centurion peered at him for a long time. 'All right then. Get your kit together and let's move out.'

CHAPTER EIGHTEEN

The guards swung open the gates and the cohort moved out. Raven felt almost as strange leaving the fort as he had when he had first entered it with his mother.

The fort had been his home and the legion had become his family – or at least as close to family as he had now. He had eaten and slept with these men for months now.

The men marched at a steady pace. The air was cold and their breath rose in puffs of thin white steam. The sky above them was pale blue and scattered with white clouds.

Raven was surprised to feel nervous about leaving the fort. Had he really been among these people for so long that he now feared his own land? Had he been enclosed by walls so long that he feared the wide horizon?

But the truth was that it was not his land any more. His people were either dead or living with other tribes. For all he knew he was the last of his kin.

When they reached the top of a hill, Raven looked back towards the wall and the fort. They seemed so small, just as they had when he had first come this way with his mother.

What was he now? Was he a Roman? He did not feel like one. He was landless and homeless.

The centurion seemed to read his thoughts as he rode alongside him. 'Strange, isn't it?' he said.

'Sir?' asked Raven.

'How quickly it becomes normal,' he said. 'The fort, the way of life?'

'Yes, sir,' he said. 'It is.'

'It's been the same for all of us, lad,' he said. 'We were all barbarians once. I am one of the few men in the fort who has ever seen Rome – and none of us were born there.'

Raven nodded. The Roman Empire was like some great rolling cloak, covering all people in its path. Soon the whole world would be Roman. And then what?

The soldiers moved on. Raven had trained long and hard in the fort but nothing quite prepared him for a Roman march, weighed down with armour and equipment. He wondered what would happen if they met the enemy at the end of the day when they would be barely able to stand. His shoulders and legs already ached.

The steady clank of the armour and thud of their feet were the only sounds for miles around, and the beat of it became a second heartbeat for Raven. Clank. Thud. Clank. Thud. On and on and on.

But Roman soldier or not, Raven's instincts as a warrior and a hunter were at full force. His eyes flickered back and forth, scanning the horizon for any sign of movement. However much he looked, though, Raven saw nothing save scattered flocks of crows and starlings hunting for berries.

As the light began to fade, they made camp. They put up tents and built fires. All the while, the centurion was allotting them tasks and calling out orders.

Raven could see that the centurion was trying to keep everyone busy so that they would not think about the dangers all around them. It was a long time before they stopped to eat, exhausted and hungry.

The warm food revived them and they settled down, staring into the fire and trying to ignore the night sounds around them.

'Look at you,' the centurion said to the soilders. 'You stare into that fire as though it was your funeral pyre. I'm not ready to die yet.'

'But, sir,' said one of the soldiers, 'can I speak freely?'

'Of course,' replied the centurion.

'Well, sir,' he said. 'We move further and further from our supplies and any chance of help. We are so few and we do not know the strength of the enemy.'

Raven looked at the centurion, who nodded and threw the remnants of his soup on to the fire with a hiss. 'That's true,' he replied, 'and I won't pretend that all of us will make it back to the fort. But I swear to you that I have hope. A soldier must always have hope.'

The soldiers looked at each other through the flames, perhaps searching for signs of hope in the faces of their comrades. Raven could see fear and tension in their eyes.

'The enemy will see us before we see them,' continued the centurion. 'Because we are out in the open and exposed, it's true. But that is our best chance.'

Raven frowned, confused. The centurion continued. 'Our best hope is to encourage them to attack us in the open. The better our view of them, the better our chance of coming through this alive.

'They act as individuals,' he said, with a brief glance at Raven that no one saw but him. 'They do not fight for each other. They fight for their own glory. That is their weakness.'

The centurion stared away into the blackness. 'A fatal weakness.'

CHAPTER
NINETEEN

None of the soldiers slept well. Raven had been woken before dawn to take his shift as guard. He stood at the fire's edge thinking what a target he was for anyone out there.

It was cold. The frosts had not arrived yet, but it was damp and chilly. The freezing air burned the back of Raven's throat as he yawned. It seemed ages before light broke over the eastern lowlands and the camp was roused to gather itself and move off.

They decamped with as much speed and efficiency as they had pitched camp. Within minutes of waking, the soldiers were on the march again.

They moved along a trackway that took them across a high moor. There had been mutterings for some time about where it was that Raven was leading them, but now the centurion voiced his concerns.

'What makes you think they've come this way?' asked the centurion. 'There are no tracks.'

'I'm trying to cut them off,' said Raven. 'It's the only chance we have of catching up with them. They could not bring the chariots this way, it's too narrow. But they are heading towards those hills, I know it. And they won't think we'd be crazy enough to follow.'

The centurion nodded.

The men continued along the ridge and then down a winding path that led to a flat boggy area. Raven pointed to the ground. There were tracks of wheels and hooves and feet.

The centurion went down on his haunches. 'Fresh,' he said. 'Can't be more than a day old – maybe less.'

The soldiers had more faith in Raven now as they looked down at the tracks running through the mud at their feet, but it only served to remind them that the fight was close.

The tracks eventually led on to another, broader path that ran north into the highlands away in the mist. It curved in a wide arc for a mile or more before entering the woods.

The centurion called for them to halt as they approached. The woods were too wide to go round and yet they provided an enemy with all the cover they needed.

'Eyes and ears open,' said the centurion. His voice was quiet but the air was so still that every man heard him. 'I need a volunteer. I need someone to walk through the woods and check that the tracks go all the way through.'

A soldier stepped forward and the centurion clapped him on the back.

'Good man,' he said. 'Take it slowly. The first sign of trouble, run like a hare back here. Understand?'

'Sir!'

The soldier set off. The path through the woods were wide but it curved. In no time at all the soldier disappeared from sight.

Raven and the others waited nervously, their muscles tense and tight, expecting that at any moment the soldier would appear being chased by a horde of barbarians.

But not long after he disappeared, he reappeared, calmly walking towards them.

'The tracks go straight through, sir,' said the soldier. 'The forest is not very deep and I followed the tracks out the other side and saw that they carried on. The ground is quite soft and the tracks are clear.'

'Good,' said the centurion. 'Then let's move. We are losing time standing here.'

The men moved towards the woods, relieved to see, as the soldier had promised, that the tracks continued all the way through. They were in sight of the woods' end when the centurion saw Raven looking about nervously.

'What is it?' said the centurion.

'Nothing sir,' said Raven.

'Come on,' said the centurion. 'Speak to me.'

Raven shook his head. 'Something's not right,' he said after a moment.

The centurion nodded and stared off into the trees. 'I know what you mean,' he said. 'Soldier. Those tracks – were they chariot wheels and footprints or just chariot wheels and hoof prints?'

'I'm not sure, sir' replied the soldier.

'Think!'

'Wheel tracks and hoof prints, sir.'

'Gods!' said the centurion. 'They've taken the chariots through to fool us.'

He turned to the rest of the men. 'Have your wits about you. I think we may be –'

Before he could reach the end of his sentence, a spear whistled past his ear. Raven raised his shield as another flew towards his face, thudded into his shield and bounced off.

Two of the soldiers were not so quick or lucky and they dropped to the ground, howling in pain.

Barbarians attacked from either side, running out of the trees, axes whirling. Raven leapt forward. His sword struck one of the attackers between his ribs. The man looked at Raven as he rammed the sword home. But as quickly as the attack started, it ended, and the barbarians melted back into the trees. There were no more Roman casualties.

'We can't fight here,' said the centurion. 'They'll pick us off, one by one. Move off! We need to find some open ground.'

'Sir – the wounded,' said one of the men. 'What about the wounded?'

'Kill them,' said the centurion.

The soldier did not move.

'Believe me; you may start wishing it were you when the fighting starts. A quick death is a good death.'

The centurion grabbed a javelin and marched forward, ramming it into the chest of the nearest wounded soldier. 'If we stay here, we will all die,' said the centurion to the rest of the men. 'And not quickly. They cannot walk and we cannot carry them and move quickly enough. If we try to take them with us, we'll all die. Now do as I ordered! If we leave them here alive, the barbarians will torture them for days before they kill them.'

After a moment the soldier who had hesitated before walked over to the wounded soldier. The soldier on the ground looked up and nodded.

The soldier leaned forward and buried his sword in the man's chest.

'Right!' said the centurion. 'Move out!'

The men did not pause this time but moved off towards the east where they could see that the forest ended.

Raven looked over his shoulder as he ran and saw barbarians move forward to the fallen men. The centurion was right. They were probably the lucky ones.

CHAPTER TWENTY

The ravine behind the soldiers meant that the enemy could not creep round and outflank them. But it also meant that they had nowhere to go.

Raven could hear the breathing of the men around him and the whispered prayers. This patch of ground was going to be the end for some of these men – maybe all of them.

'All is not lost, men' said the centurion. 'The enemy think they have us beaten, but if they want my life they are still going to have to come and take it from me!

'Remember your training,' he continued. 'Hold your nerve and wait for my orders. Listen to me and only me – not the little voice in your head or the ghost of your ancestor. Just me.'

No sooner had he said this than there was some movement among the barbarians. One of their number strode forward – a giant of a man, Raven could see, even from that distance.

He began to swing something round his head. Raven wondered what kind of weapon this could be and steadied himself.

The giant released his missile and it flew threw the air to bounce once and land about six feet from the Roman soldiers. It was a Roman helmet, and as it hit the ground, the head it contained rolled out.

There were groans even from the older soldiers and Raven struggled to turn his face away, recognising the man whose head now lay in the dirt staring towards him.

'Eyes front!' shouted the centurion. 'Don't let these swine break you. That soldier has gone to the gods. If you don't want to join him, then keep your wits about you.'

The barbarians had cheered and jeered as the head had hit the ground, and the giant went back to the rest of his clan to much back-slapping and laughter. The centurion leaned towards Raven.

'Can you hit him?' he asked.

'Yes, sir,' said Raven, still trying to take his eyes off the severed head.

'Do it,' said the centurion.

Raven kept low and backed away from the rest of the men, picking up a javelin as he did so and peering at the giant, who was stepping back with a second head.

Raven worked out the distance between him and the target, allowing for the ground dropping away and the slight breeze that gusted every now and then.

When the giant began to swing the helmet above his own head, Raven stood up and marched forward, trailing the javelin behind him before launching it into the air.

The head left the giant's hands just as the javelin struck him in the chest, the point driving clean through him and knocking him backwards, pinning him to the ground. The point of the javelin crumpled under his weight and he collapsed on to the grass, coughing blood.

Instead of cheers and laughter, the barbarians now cursed and shouted, waving their axes at the Romans. One of them rushed forward, spear in hand, hurling it towards them, but it landed harmlessly yards away.

'Now they'll come,' said the centurion. 'Get ready. They are many and we are few. Our only chance is as a group. Fight on your own and we will all die.'

The centurion was looking at Raven as he spoke these words and Raven nodded. 'Sir,' he said.

The barbarians gathered together and began to chant and howl; it sounded so strange and unearthly in that wild and empty place. It silenced the rooks and seemed to still the wind. Again Raven heard the muttered prayers and oaths of his comrades.

Then the barbarians' chief walked through his men and stood in front of them. Raven could see the torc shining at his throat.

'This is it,' said the centurion. 'This is it.'

And sure enough the chieftain raised his axe and his head and howled like a wolf until the rest of the men grew silent and the howl was the only sound. Then he lowered his head and started to walk forward.

A great yell went up from the barbarians as they followed their chief, first walking, then running. The Romans did not move a muscle. The enemy had already halved the distance between them

'Now!' shouted the centurion.

Raven and three other men stood up and hurled javelins at the onrushing men. All three struck true and the men fell backwards, but it did not slow the attack for even a second.

'Defence!' yelled the centurion, and the soldiers gathered into the tortoise in a heartbeat.

In moments the barbarians were on them, battering into the shield with a noise like thunder, but that sound was soon joined by cries of pain as the Romans jabbed their swords from between the shields and into the flesh of their attackers.

Raven saw the chief smashing his axe against the shield next to him. It took all of his will not to turn away from his own opponent and attack his father's killer.

The jabbing, hacking shield wall of the Romans was merciless. The barbarians lost their nerve and were forced to run away, led by their chief. One of the Romans began to cheer, but the centurion struck him on the armour plating on his shoulder. 'No!' he said. 'This is not a rabble. This is the Roman army. Anyone wounded?'

'Sir,' replied three men.

'You,' he said to one of the other men. 'Check their wounds. Do what you can and get them back in line.'

'Sir,' said the soldier.

'You, you and you,' said the centurion. 'Finish them off.'

The centurion had included Raven in that and he pointed to the fallen barbarians who lay groaning and crawling on the ground.

'Sir,' said the soldiers. Raven had not replied.

'Move it, soldier,' said the centurion to Raven.

'Sir,' said Raven, getting up and walking to the nearest man, who lay there clutching a wound in his side and whimpering. He could not have been much older than Raven.

'Please,' he said as he saw Raven steady himself with his sword. Raven thought of his father and of his village. He looked towards the chief who stared back with his men. Then he leaned forward and rammed his sword into the man's heart.

An angry roar came from the bottom of the ravine when the barbarians realised what the Romans were doing. Raven looked down at the chieftain and they seemed to have eye contact for a few seconds.

The enemy attacked again. They roared up the slope like a stampede of horses, snorting and grunting, their eyes wide and wild.

But the fight and the hill were taking their toll. Raven saw that the effort was greater now, their movements slower and heavier. By the time they reached the Roman line, they were gasping for breath.

Then the centurion gave the order. 'Forward!'

The Romans formed the wedge now and lurched forward to meet their attackers, catching them by surprise.

The wedge was like a terrible machine, grinding its way through the enemy, jabbing and hacking.

Just as he had been trained, Raven went for anything he could see, slashing at legs, arms – whatever came in view. It was brutal and without mercy, but it was effective.

He understood now that this was not cowardice. It took all his willpower not to break free and fight on his own. Each man was forced to rely on the man next to him. If one man failed – they all would feel the effect.

The attackers began to lose heart. Hampered by wound after wound, they tried again and again to break the Roman defence, howling in pain and fury, but time and again they failed. Soon they began to limp away.

As soon as the barbarians turned, the centurion gave the order and they were up and after them, hacking them down.

Raven looked around for the red-haired chief and saw him running for his chariot. He uncoupled one of the horses and jumped on to its back.

Raven cursed. His father would never have left his men and run from the field of battle. Raven could not believe that his father's murderer was going to escape again.

As the chief kicked his heels and set off, Raven turned and saw his chance. All his training as a soldier of Rome was forgotten in that instant. He ran to uncouple the other horse.

'What are you doing, soldier?' asked the centurion.

'I have to get him, sir,' said Raven.

'You have to stay here,' said the centurion, grabbing his arm.

Raven turned, sword ready. The centurion backed off, glaring at him.

'Don't try to stop me.'

'I'm going to –'

But the centurion never finished what he was saying because a barbarian behind him struck him in the head with the handle of an axe and he dropped to the ground.

Raven grabbed the barbarian's axe hand before he struck again and punched his sword between his ribs.

Raven hesitated for a moment, looking down at the centurion but then mounted the horse. He turned to see his comrades hacking down the attackers. They were winning. They could manage without him. He jabbed his heels into the horse and rode after the chieftain.

CHAPTER
TWENTY-ONE

Raven never took his eyes from the chief. He knew that if he lost him, even for a moment, he might hide anywhere and Raven would never know when the man might leap out at him.

They rode on. On and on and on. The drum of the hooves on the track and the wind in his face sent Raven into a kind of trance. Nothing seemed to exist in the whole wide world except for him and the man he chased.

Raven knew that what he was doing was foolish. He was following a man into a land he did not know. For all he knew he was being led into a trap and the first he would know it was when an arrow or spear hit his heart.

But he had no choice. He could no more let his father's killer escape than he could go back in time and prevent his death. The gods had given him one more chance at revenge and he might not get another.

On and on they rode. Raven felt the spirit of his father at his side urging him to go faster. He jabbed his heels and pleaded with his horse to speed up.

The horse was willing but Raven could feel it getting tired beneath him. He could hear its wheezing breath and sense its tired limbs and sore muscles.

These horses were meant for pulling work. They could trot for hours with a chariot behind them. They were strong horses with big hearts, but they were not made for the gallop. But just as he could tell that his horse was tiring, he knew too that the chieftain's horse ahead of him was tiring too.

But Raven guessed that the chieftain had not chosen his horse at random; for though both horses were slowing, Raven's horse seemed to be slowing more and the chieftain's horse was, for the first time, widening the gap between them.

Raven cursed and jabbed his heels into the horse, but he knew that the animal was going as fast as it could. If he pushed it much harder, the beast would collapse under him.

Was this really going to be the end? Was he really going to lose sight of his father's killer in this wild place and ride back to live on with this memory?

Raven cursed again and felt his horse slowing, its movements becoming heavier and heavier, when suddenly up ahead he saw something that made his heart sing.

The chieftain had worked his horse hard for too long. Raven saw the horse's legs buckle under its body and it fell to the ground, throwing the rider.

The chief got up and shook his head and looked back at the approach of Raven and ran off through the heather towards the nearby hills.

Raven rode on until he reached the fallen horse and then dismounted. The horse was gasping and kicking its legs, as though still running. Its eyes were wild and its spirit seemed already to have left its body.

He set out after the chief. The tall figure with his long red hair was easy enough to spot among the dark heather in the shadow of the hill.

He had already started to climb the hill when Raven reached across the heather and bog that lay between them. And by the time Raven was at the hill's foot, the chief was a small shadow above him.

The hill was steeper than it looked from the track. It was more of a cliff made up of boulders and an open rock face and loose stones. Raven had already discarded his body armour and shoulder plates, but as the barbarian above him turned back to look at him, Raven took off his helmet and threw it aside.

Even from that distance Raven saw the smile on the barbarian's face as he realised the youth of the man who had been chasing him.

Raven's mouth was dry and he stopped for a moment to drink some ice-cold water from a nearby brook. Then he carried on.

CHAPTER
TWENTY-TWO

Raven climbed. The way was steep and loose under foot and Raven knew that the chief wanted him to exhaust himself on the ascent. He needed to pace himself. He must go as slowly as he needed. There was time.

When he reached the top, he saw that they stood at the edge of a great cleft in the rock where a stream, bulging with the water from the recent rain, rolled over boulders far below.

The cut in which the waterfall roared was narrow and steep. The chief stood on the other side and smiled at Raven, who stood panting, hands on hips and head bowed.

'Come, Roman,' said the chief. 'I could have killed you as you climbed, but I will give you the honour of combat.'

'I am *not* Roman,' said Raven. He showed the chief his tattoos.

'You are a traitor!' yelled the chief.

'You are a murderer!' called Raven in return. 'You killed my father, coward!'

'You dare call me coward, boy?' he called back above the roar of the waterfall.

'My father was a great warrior and he deserved a warrior's death,' said Raven. 'But you killed him like a dog.'

'Your father was a fool. And he has fathered a fool. Look at you. You scarcely have breath to stand.'

Raven panted for a while longer and then his breathing slowly calmed. He raised his head and looked at the chieftain's face and saw it twitch as the man realised that Raven had only been pretending to be exhausted.

Raven leapt over the waterfall and carried on running, striking the chief as he did so, his sword clanging against the chieftain's axe.

The chief immediately hit back, his axe whistling past Raven's ear. He struck out again and Raven barely managed to duck in time.

Raven lunged forward, thrusting the point of his sword towards the chief's belly, but the warrior was ready for him and struck him on the side of his face with his fist.

Raven stumbled, almost falling into the raging waterfall. The chief stepped forward and kicked him. Raven slipped and slid over the wet stones.

He cried out, just managing to grab hold of a rock and stop himself from falling over.

The chief grinned down at him. 'Did you really think you could defeat me, boy? Look at you! Beg me for your life and I might take pity on you.'

Raven knew full well that the chief had no intention of sparing him no matter what he said. The chief stamped on Raven's arm. The pain almost made him let go, but he clung on.

'Beg for your life!' yelled the chief, his voice echoing around the rocks.

Raven was busily scrabbling with his feet and suddenly found a ledge near his shins. He put his foot on it without the chief seeing.

'Then die!' said the chief.

He raised his axe over his head and Raven launched himself upward at the instant the chief was about to bring his weapon crashing down, ramming his sword into the chief's gut.

The chief sank to his knees, dropping his axe and grabbing the sword hilt with his hands, as if trying to pull it out.

Raven clambered over the rocks and picked up the chief's axe. The chief turned to face him, a look of calm acceptance on his face. Raven swung the axe.

CHAPTER
TWENTY-THREE

Raven was exhausted from the chase and from the fight. He slept in a cave beneath a crag, cold water seeping through the cracks in the rocks and dripping with a steady meter through the night.

Raven's father had taught him to always carry flint and some dry moss and he was glad that he had not stopped doing that even in the Roman army.

He managed to find enough dry kindling to start a fire and wrapped himself in the dead chief's cloak and stared into the flames.

The fire brought back memories of the one that warmed the round house in his village as the sparks danced in the blackness. He remembered how as a child he would see all kinds of creatures coil and flicker in its flames, the heat so strong it hurt his eyes to watch for long. But there were no dragons in these flames. This was a fire and nothing more. Even its warmth did not seem the same. The warmth inside had come from the people around him. People who were lost to him now.

He pulled the cloak round him a little more and as he saw the cloth – the kind of cloth his mother might have made – he wondered what he was now. He wondered where – if anywhere – he truly belonged.

He woke to a crisp clear dawn with birds calling from a small knot of wind-twisted trees above him. He stretched his arms and winced as cuts opened and bruised muscles strained.

He went to the stream and gasped as he put his arm into the cold, clear water that bit into his flesh like teeth.

He washed away the dried blood and the cold numbed the pain a little. He splashed water on his face; it felt good.

Sun sparkled across the water as it disappeared over the edge and between the smooth round boulders. It seemed such a different place from the one he had seen yesterday.

Before he left the waterfall, Raven dragged the body of the chief to the edge. He stared down at it for a long time, disappointed that it did not feel as good as he had hoped to look down on the corpse of his father's murderer.

The wind picked up and shook the leaves of a nearby birch tree, making then shimmer and whisper. Raven suddenly felt alone – terribly alone.

With a muttered curse, he kicked the body of the chief into the ravine where it disappeared into the foam and spray and rocks below.

'Let your stinking spirit stay there forever,' he said.

Raven stood there for a long time, staring into the bubbling water. He had thought that he would feel happier but he did not. If anything he felt emptier. His quest for revenge had given a meaning to his life. Now he had nothing.

Raven retraced his steps down the hillside and found his horse nearby. Its ears pricked at his approach and it looked happy to see some sign of life in that wasteland.

Raven patted the horse on the neck and it nuzzled into him. This small show of affection from the horse was too much for Raven and he began to sob, burying his face into the horse's mane, remembering his own horse, Storm, and the way of life that went with it.

All the pain of the last years seemed to rise up inside him and he hugged the horse and cried until his body felt weak and his head dizzy.

Slowly Raven raised his head and looked around him, his tears drying on his cheeks. He mounted the horse, took one look back towards the waterfall and rode away.

CHAPTER
TWENTY-FOUR

At first Raven rode with no great sense of direction other than to ride south and away from enemy land. In the end he knew he had little choice but to return to the fort. For better or worse, the soldiers were all he had now. He had no idea what would happen to him for deserting the others, but he was sure that he would be allowed to return.

Raven rode for hours, using the sun as his guide. He knew that he would eventually meet the wall and that he could find the fort from there.

He walked along a high ridge that had wide sweeping views across the moors and hills. From behind one hill he saw a huge column of smoke rising and decided he ought to find out what it was.

Another hour found him standing on a low hillside looking down on a scene that seemed horribly familiar.

A village was being attacked. Raven guessed it must be Redwing's. Screaming woman ran this way and that. Children huddled to their mothers. Men begged for mercy. But the Romans spared no one.

The reinforcements the commander had promised had clearly moved north and gone to the enemy village while the bulk of the warriors were away.

Raven turned and rode on before he was seen. Instead of continuing due south to the wall, Raven headed west towards his old village and arrived as the light faded.

The village was overgrown now. Weeds smothered the remains of the houses and small trees were growing through the roofs. It looked as though it had not been lived in for centuries.

Raven lit a fire in the ruin of the great round house in which he had heard so many tales and went to the stream to catch fish with a wooden spear, as his father had taught him to do many years before.

He slept and dreamt about the round house as it was in happy days, a fire burning, the smell of meat roasting, the sound of laughter and good cheer. He dreamt he saw his father and mother break off from their talk and look across at him and smile as if they were saying goodbye.

In the morning Raven strode over to the barrow where his father's ashes were buried. He dug away at the entrance with his bare hands, pulling up the mud and turf until the stones were exposed and then he moved those, stacking them in a neat pile nearby.

He leaned forward to put the Dragonhead Torc inside the burial chamber, but just as he did so, a raven – the bird he had been named for – swooped down and landed on top of the barrow, croaking.

Raven looked up, startled. The black bird stood in front of the sun and Raven had to squint to look at him. The raven croaked again and he seemed to hear his father's voice.

'Keep it,' it said. 'The torc is yours now.'

'Father?'

The bird took to the air, flying away to the hills with long lazy wing beats.

'Keep it, keep it!' it croaked. 'Torc! Torc!'

Raven looked at the torc in his hands and the gold seemed to catch the sunlight. It felt warm. He looked once more to the raven, now a black speck in the distance, and put the torc behind his neck, pushing it round until the great dragon heads met at the front.

CHAPTER
TWENTY–FIVE

Raven walked into the fort with the chief's cloak round him and the sentries did not recognise him. He had stayed almost a week in his old village, but somehow he felt he had to return. Despite everything, the fort was home. If he belonged anywhere now, he belonged here.

The first thing he did was to seek out his comrades in his century and find out what happened. They were astonished to see him.

'They've locked up the centurion,' they told him. 'He is to be executed for failing to capture the enemy leader.'

'I don't think so,' said Raven.

Raven arrived at the commander's house with a small guard of soldiers on either side. The commander walked out to meet him.

'Well then,' he said. 'You have returned.'

'Yes, sir,' said Raven.

'Why?' said the commander in a bored voice. 'Why come back? You are a deserter and you will be punished as a deserter. You were the murderer I pardoned, weren't you? This is what happens when we are lenient. Perhaps I will crucify you after all.' The commander smiled at this thought.

'I am a loyal Roman, sir,' said Raven.

'I doubt that,' said the commander with the raise of an eyebrow.

'The centurion sent me on a mission, sir,' said Raven.

'The centurion?' said the commander. 'Dear me, but you have made a grave mistake if you expect the centurion to look after you. He is in the jailhouse himself.'

'I know nothing of that, sir,' said Raven. 'Has he committed some crime?'

'He has failed the Emperor!' shouted the commander. 'There is no crime more serious than that!'

Raven made no reply.

'What was this mission?' asked the commander.

'He sent me to seek out the leader of the barbarians and kill him, sir,' said Raven. 'As you yourself ordered.'

'He sent you … alone?' asked the commander. 'Why would he do that?'

'Because he knew that only I could track him in this country as it is my native land.'

'And did you kill him?'

'Yes, sir,' answered Raven.

The commander raised an eyebrow again and looked at the assembled soldiers. 'And we just have to take your word for it, do we?'

'No, sir,' said Raven and handed him a leather bag.

The commander looked puzzled, then opened the bag and immediately dropped it, staggering back and retching. The barbarian's head rolled loose, tangled in red hair.

'This means nothing!' hissed the commander. 'You are still a deserter.'

The soldiers in the garrison began to murmur.

'Be still!' shouted the commander nervously.

'Sir,' said Raven. 'You said that the man who brought back the head of the barbarian would be rewarded.'

The commander nodded, still casting a wary eye over the assembled men. 'Yes,' he said slowly, changing his mind as he looked at the crowd of soldiers. 'Yes, I did.'

'Very well,' he said in a loud voice, addressing the men as much as Raven. 'Name your price and if it is within my powers to grant it, I will!'

'Release the centurion, sir,' said Raven.

The commander turned and glared at him in fury. 'You dare make such demands of me?' he said. 'I'll kill you myself.'

The commander's hand went to the hilt of his sword but so did the hand of every soldier in the fort. The commander stopped and looked around at the sea of faces that stared back. 'Archers!' shouted the commander.

Archers appeared on the ramparts of the wall and

aimed their arrows. Initially they all aimed them at the soldiers below, but slowly they turned to point them at the commander instead.

'What is this?' demanded the commander. 'I'll have you all crucified. I'll send to Rome and –'

'We are loyal servants of Rome, sir,' said Raven. 'And so is the centurion.'

The commander looked at the troops and chewed on the inside of his lips for a while. He looked at Raven and then at the archers.

'Release the centurion,' he said.

CHAPTER
TWENTY-SIX

The centurion was released and, despite the fact that he knew Raven was responsible, he made a point of telling him never to disobey his orders again.

'I haven't forgotten about what happened back there,' he said. 'If I hadn't been knocked out …'

'I'm sorry, sir,' said Raven.

'You don't look sorry,' said the centurion with a smile. 'The men brought me back to the fort and the commander immediately locked me up.'

Raven shook his head.

'What is that?' said the centurion, pointing at Raven's neck.

'It is the Dragonhead Torc,' replied Raven. 'It belonged to my father. It was taken by the man I killed. If he had taken it by true contest, it would be his by right. But he killed my father in a cowardly manner and so it did not belong to him.'

'And does it belong to you?' asked the centurion.

Raven thought about this for a moment and nodded. 'Yes,' he said. 'I think it does. My father won it by combat and now I have done the same. It feels right. It feels like I've earned it.'

The centurion nodded. 'I think you have.'

Raven had earned his place in the legion as well. A ceremony was held at which he was led blindfold into the temple and had his hand tattooed with the eagle, swearing that he would defend the honour of the legion with his life.

'You already have,' said the centurion when they had finished.

As for the commander, he was not seen very often after that. He began to be obsessed about being stabbed or shot by an arrow if he left his quarters.

He trusted no one and lost weight. He began to worry that his precious wine and olives would be poisoned and, even though he had a slave taste every glass and every olive before he did, they still tasted bitter to him and he could not enjoy them.

'The commander has finally got his wish,' said the centurion one day to Raven. 'He is being posted back to Rome.'

'How did that happen?'

The centurion smiled and looked to make sure there was no one within listening range.

'I still have some friends in Rome,' he said. 'I explained that the commander might be happier nearer the Emperor. His replacement arrives next month.'

Raven looked towards the commander's house. 'It seems unfair in a way,' he said. 'It feels like he is being rewarded.'

'He might come to regret it,' said the centurion. 'People like to be close to power because they do not want to be out in the cold. But it can be too hot. Get too close to a man like Commodus and it's only a matter of time before you get burned.'

Raven nodded, although he found it hard to imagine what Rome or Commodus could possibly be like.

'There is something else,' said the centurion. 'There was a price for getting the commander moved.'

'Sir?' said Raven.

'I am to be posted back to Rome myself,' said the centurion. 'The senator who helped me with the commander thinks that it might be a good time for trustworthy men to be brought back to Rome.'

Raven nodded. 'Good luck, sir,' he said.

'I think I may need someone to watch my back when I'm there. How would you like to come with me?'

Raven stared in amazement, half expecting this last statement to be a joke at his expense.

'I'm serious, boy. When the new commander arrives, I will be recommending you for a promotion. What do you say?'

Raven frowned. Rome was little more than a word to him. He had no real idea of what it must be like.

He looked at the fort and the wall and tried to imagine his homeland beyond. Then he looked to the south, to the lands that were a mystery to him.

'Yes,' he said. 'Yes, sir. I will come with you.'

The centurion clapped him on the back. 'Good lad.'

'Rome?' said Raven, shaking his head, still trying to come to terms with such an adventure. 'But what will we do there, sir?'

'Whatever we are told,' said the centurion with a smile.

THE END

Tougher Than a Roman Soldier?

By Christopher Edge

Putting history's greatest warriors to the test

Training to be a Roman soldier was a tough life, but did that make Roman soldiers the toughest soldiers? Let's look back through history to try to find the toughest warriors of all time. We'll look at their training, the weapons they used and the battles they fought. Only then will we be able to say which warriors are the toughest.

Roman Legionary

Soldiers in the Roman army were called legionaries. Only fit and healthy men who were between twenty and fourty-five years old were allowed to join the army.

Training

New recruits started with three months' basic training. This included:

- learning how to fight using different weapons;
- marching for twenty miles in full armour;
- running, swimming and horse riding.

Recruits would fight each other using wooden swords and shields to practise hand-to-hand combat. These practice weapons were much heavier than real swords and shields.

This meant that when recruits had to fight for real they were much faster fighters because they were used to using heavier weapons.

Weapons

Roman soldiers used two main weapons:

- the javelin: a special spear which was thrown at enemy soldiers;
- the gladius: a short sword used in hand-to-hand combat.

Roman soldiers also used bows and arrows, daggers and darts when fighting. For protection they used shields and wore helmets and body armour. This armour was made out of strips of metal which were flexible and easy to fight in.

Battles

The Roman army fought thousands of battles across Europe, the Middle East and Africa. Their skill as soldiers made the Roman army one of the most feared armies in the world.

Spartan Warrior

In Ancient Greece, the city state of Sparta was ruled by fierce warriors – the Spartans. Every Spartan man served as a full-time soldier, spending his whole life training and fighting.

Training

At the age of seven, Spartan boys were taken away from their parents. They were made to live in barracks where they were trained for battle. They learned:

- sword fighting;
- discus and javelin throwing;

- boxing and wrestling.

Life was hard. Boys were given few clothes to wear and were kept cold and hungry. If they were caught stealing food, they were whipped. This punishment wasn't for stealing, but for being caught. This meant the boys hadn't learned the stealth and cunning a Spartan soldier needed. Those who survived to the age of twenty were then made to join the army as Spartan warriors.

Weapons

Like the Roman soldier, the sword and the spear were the main weapons that Spartan warriors fought with. However, a Spartan spear wasn't used for throwing. Instead, this long stabbing spear called a *dory* was used to break through an enemy army's shields. The spear had a large spike at the bottom of its shaft. This was used to finish off enemy soldiers as they lay wounded on the ground.

If a Spartan warrior's spear broke in battle, he would draw his sword. There were two main types of sword:

- the *xiphos*: a very short sword with a lethal double-edged blade;
- the *kiros*: a curved sword used for hacking and slashing in close combat.

With whichever weapon he chose, a Spartan warrior was a deadly fighter.

Battles

The most famous battle fought by the Spartans was the Battle of Thermopylae. In this battle 300 Spartans fought against an army of 250,000 Persian soldiers! The Spartans were defending a narrow mountain pass against the invading Persian army. For three days, the Spartans held back the Persians until the 300 warriors were finally defeated and killed.

Samurai Swordsman

For many hundreds of years, the samurai were the most feared warriors in Japan. Brave and skilled swordsmen, the samurai followed the 'Way of the Warrior'. This meant that they swore absolute loyalty to their lord and master and would die in battle for him.

Training

Children as young as five could be chosen to train as a samurai. They were sent away to training camps where they learned:

- sword fighting;
- martial arts;
- archery;
- horse riding.

As well as the skills they would use in battle, samurai were also taught history, poetry and art. It was important to train a samurai's mind as well as his body.

Weapons

A samurai's main weapon was his sword. Called a *katana*, this sword had a sharp curved blade, which could cut a man's head off with a single blow. This was the punishment given to any cowardly soldiers who tried to run away from battle.

As well as his sword, a samurai warrior could also use the following weapons:

- the *bō*: a long wooden staff that could be used in hand-to-hand combat
- the *kanabō*: a heavy club with iron spikes at one end
- the *tantō*: a sharp dagger
- the *yari*: a long spear
- the *yumi*: a longbow.

To protect himself in battle, a samurai wore a metal helmet and a suit of plate armour.

Battles

In the time of the samurai, Japan was a country at war with itself. Rival warlords ruled different parts of the country. Each warlord had their own army of samurai. Many battles were fought among the samurai as the rival warlords tried to take control of the whole country.

Viking Berserker

The Vikings were pirates from Northern Europe who lived in medieval times. They raided and invaded many countries, stealing gold, silver, land and women.

Training

Vikings were master sailors who could travel great distances in their longships. They learned their fighting skills from a young age by hunting and taking part in raids. If a young Viking warrior showed courage in battle, he would be rewarded with treasure.

The most feared Viking warrior was the berserker. This was the name given to warriors who worked themselves up into a terrible rage before a battle. They wore cloaks made out of bearskins and fought like wild animals. Stories say that berserkers had the strength of ten men and didn't feel any pain at all. Not the kind of person you want to meet in a fight!

Weapons

Vikings fought with spears, swords and battleaxes.

- Spears were used for throwing and stabbing. This was the most common Viking weapon because it was the cheapest to make.
- Only the most powerful Viking warriors would own a sword. These swords were given names such as Leg-biter and Viper.
- The scariest Viking weapon was the battleaxe. This could split a shield in two as well as chop your head off!

Battles

Vikings loved to fight. From a single ship of looting raiders to a great army of thousands of men, the Vikings were feared wherever they went.

Decision time

Who do you think is the toughest warrior from history? Roman legionary or Viking berserker? Spartan or samurai? As Harry Hill would say, there's only one way to find out – fight!

We would like to thank the following schools and students for all their help in developing and trialling *Blood Oath*.

Croesyceiliog School, Cwmbran

Callum Beckett

Josh Tyler

Ryan Lo

Hannah Evans

Ben Hobby

Huish Episcopi Academy, Somerset

Blake Armstrong

Tom Levett

Ben Lock

Charlie Stamp

Michael Tew

Jack Stephens